Beautiful Stories for Children

CHRISTIAN LIBERTY PRESS

ARLINGTON HEIGHTS, ILLINOIS

A publication of
Christian Liberty Press
502 West Euclid Avenue
Arlington Heights, Illinois 60004

Revised by: Michael J. McHugh
Editor: Edward J. Shewan
Proofreader: Diane C. Olson

CHRISTIAN LIBERTY PRESS
502 West Euclid Avenue
Arlington Heights, Illinois 60004
www.christianlibertypress.com

ISBN 978-1-930092-31-8
       1-930092-31-0

Printed in the United States of America

PREFACE

We encourage teachers to use *Beautiful Stories for Children* with students in the primary grades, especially beginning with the second grade. This particular reader is designed to improve the reading skills and comprehension of those students.

To be able to read is to have the foundation for all subsequent education. The child whose literacy training is deficient may become frustrated and desperate, which may lead to problems in other areas of life.

As we look at the readers of days gone by we find that the biblical standard was followed. Such readers featured the finest British and American authors who emphasized God, morality, the wonders of creation, and respect for one's country. *Beautiful Stories for Children* seeks to follow this pattern of the past.

Most lessons begin with a list of vocabulary words, which the teacher should go over with the student. Once the child learns their pronunciations and meanings, the student may begin reading the story or poem that follows.

It is our prayer that this book will give children the joy that is to be associated with "good reading," and that the knowledge imparted will help "make wise the simple" (Psalm 19:7).

Michael J. McHugh
Christian Liberty Press
2003

Contents

Lesson 1

scholar—pupil; learner
teacher—one who teaches; instructor
through—to the end
mean—stand for
study—use one's mind to learn
correctly—right; as it should be
difficult—hard; not easy
marks—periods (.), commas (,), semi-colons (;),
       hyphens (-), em dashes (—)
pauses—stops; rests

The Good Scholars

Emma: Teacher, may Charles and I each have a new book? We have read this book through three times.

Teacher: Do you think you can spell all the words in that book, and tell me what they mean?

Emma: I think we can spell them all correctly; but I do not know if we can tell you what they all mean.

Teacher: Well, Emma, please spell the word "guilt," and tell me what it means.

Emma: G-u-i-l-t—guilt; it means "shame."

Teacher: Charles, please spell "neat."

Charles: N-e-a-t—neat; it means "in order."

Teacher: Very well. Emma, you may spell "catch."

Emma: C-a-t-c-h—catch; "to take hold of."

Teacher: Charles, you may spell "climb."

Charles: C-l-i-m-b—climb; "to go up."

Teacher: Very well done. You shall each have a new book. But you will have to study, because you will find that some words are difficult in this book.

Emma: Thank you, Teacher. When we get through this book, we will try to spell them all and tell you what they mean.

Teacher: Yes; but you will have to learn how to say each word correctly. You will also need to learn how marks and pauses are used.

Charles: Emma, I think we can learn them, too, if we study hard.

Teacher: I am sure you will both do your best for God's glory.

LESSON 2

hunt—look for; search
caught—trapped; seized
started— began; set out
quarrel—fight; dispute
wished—desired
struggle—contest; strife
blame—find fault with
sorry—grieved
cruel—unfeeling
wicked—sinful

The Boys and the Bird's Nest

Two boys, who were brothers, went into the woods one day to hunt for a bird's nest. After looking for some time, they found one on a low branch of a tree, with a bird on the nest.

One boy crept up behind the tree and caught the bird before it could fly from the nest. The other boy took the nest, which had four blue eggs in it. Then they both started for home.

While they were on their way, the boys began to quarrel about the bird; for they both wished to have it. During the struggle, the bird flew away, and the boys stepped on the nest and broke the bird's eggs. The boys then began to argue and blame each other for the loss of the bird and its nest of eggs.

When the boys returned home, their mother asked them to tell her what they had been doing and why they were arguing. The boys told her how they had taken the bird with its nest of eggs and how they had began to quarrel.

Their mother said, "My sons, I am sorry that you have been so cruel and wicked. It is cruel to rob a bird of its nest, and it is wicked for brothers to quarrel."

Both of these boys failed to remember that the Bible directs us to be slow to anger. The Book of Proverbs tells us that, "He that is slow to anger is better than the mighty; and he that ruleth his spirit than he that taketh a city." (Proverbs 16:32)

LESSON 3

watches—looks at
except—leaving out
gently—kindly; lovingly
rough—harsh; not smooth
chase—run after
lively—active; full of life
awake—not asleep
rolled—tumbled
pulled—drew
stitches—links of yarn
nibbling—biting with small, gentle bites
fierce—cruel; terrible
ready—prepared

Sarah and Her Kittens

Sarah has a cat that has four little kittens. One is white, another is reddish-brown, and two are gray.

Sarah takes good care of them. Everyday she puts some milk in a dish and watches the kittens while they lap it up.

Her favorite kitten is a dark gray, except for a white patch around its right eye; so she calls it "Patch." When Sarah picks it up lovingly, it begins to purr and lick her hand with its rough tongue. If she holds Patch still for a while, and gently passes her hand over its back, it will fold its paws, curl itself up, and go to sleep.

When Patch is awake, it is a lively little kitten and will play with pieces of paper or anything it finds on the floor. If Sarah ties a string to a ball of yarn, and then rolls it around on the floor, Patch will chase after it, as though it were a mouse.

One day Patch got into Sarah's workbasket and rolled a ball of yarn and some spools of thread out on the floor. Then the playful kitten pulled the needles and stitches out of the scarf she was knitting. Sarah did not like what Patch did, but it made her laugh.

Patch is not old enough to hunt; but, when it hears a sound like nibbling or scratching, it will perk up its ears and look very fierce. If Sarah's dog comes into the room, the kitten will arch up its back, and raise up its hair, as though it were very angry—getting ready to fight. God has surely made kittens a lot of fun and very interesting.

Lesson 4

near—close by
peep—sneak a look
called—named
broken—cracked; ruined
around—about
burst—broke forth
ruined—destroyed; broken
hatched—come out; been born
away—off

Mary and Her Bird's Nest

A bird came and built its nest in a bush, near the house where Mary lived. She would go and peep into the nest to look at the bird's little blue eggs; she called it her bird's nest.

One day her mother said, "Mary, you must not go and look at the bird's nest again for three weeks." Mary was a good girl and did as she was told. She did not go near the nest during that whole time.

After three weeks, her mother said, "Now, Mary, you may go and look at your bird's nest."

Mary ran out to the bush; but she saw nothing but broken shells all around the nest. She burst into tears, ran into the house, and said, "O mother, my little blue eggs are all ruined!"

"No, my child," said her mother, "the baby birds have hatched and flown away! After all, little baby birds cannot live forever in tiny eggshells. The birds have left their nest so they can begin to enjoy the gift of life more fully.

"Some day you will grow up and fly away from the home of your youth, like these little birds. Lord willing, you will be ready to live a wonderful life."

Lesson 5

gentle—mild; meek
allow—let happen
garden—rich spot of ground to raise fruit,
    flowers, etc.
charge—care; trust
bellow—make a loud, hollow cry
seize—catch; grasp
likely—probably
collar—neck-band
reward—repay; give a prize
faithful—loyal; trustworthy

Matt and His Dog Shadow

I will now tell you a story about Matt and his dog Shadow. Shadow was a large, strong dog; yet it was so gentle that it would let Matt jump upon its back and ride.

Shadow was a good dog to have around the house, for it would not allow the pigs and hens to go into the garden.

When Matt and his sister Ellen went out into the fields, Shadow would always go with them, as though he had the entire charge of them.

One day, as Matt and Ellen were going through a field, an angry bull began to bellow and run at them. At first, the children did not see the bull until Shadow started to bark. Then Matt yelled, "Shadow, seize it!"

Right away Shadow sprang at the bull, grabbed it by the nose, and held the bull's nose tight. Matt and Ellen ran out of the field, and then Shadow let the bull go.

After that, Matt and Ellen ran to the house and told their father what Shadow had done. Their father replied, "It was a good thing that Shadow went with you; for, if your dog had not been there, most likely you would have been killed."

"Shadow is a good dog!" cried Matt and Ellen, both at the same time.

"Yes," said their father; "and I will buy a brass

collar, and you may put it around Shadow's neck as a reward for his faithful care over you."

"We are happy that you are going to reward Shadow," said Matt, "for he is faithful."

LESSON 6

busy—active; hard-working
idle—lazy
nectar—sweet "juice" of flowers
useful—of use; helpful
gather—collect
lack—want; need
safely—free from danger
honeycomb—group of cells used to store
      honey
pollen—yellow dust on flowers
beebread—pollen and honey mixed together
excuse—reason to remove blame
benefit—be useful to
future—what is to come

The Busy Bees

All idle boys and girls can learn a useful lesson from the busy bees.

In summer, as soon as the sun rises, the bees go out to gather nectar from the flowers. They do not waste the long, sunny hours of summer; but they store up food in their hives for winter. When winter comes, they do not lack food, even though there are no flowers to give them honey.

If you go near bees in a flower garden, you will see how they gather the sweet food. When they get all the nectar they can, they fly to the hive, make honey, and store it away safely in the cells of the honeycomb.

In every hive, there are three kinds of bees. There is one large bee, which is called the queen; it rules the hive. There are also some idle bees that do little work and need to be fed; these are called drones. Most of the bees in the hive are called worker bees; they do most of the work.

The worker bees look for nectar and pollen from flowers. Then they make honey and beebread to feed to baby bees. Some workers make wax and build the cells, where babies live and honey is stored. In the fall, the worker bees push all the drones out of the hive and into the cold to die.

Do not be idle, like the lazy drones; but be like the busy worker bees that store up food for the time of need. There is no excuse for being idle. Boys and girls can always find something to do that will benefit them at some future time. It is a faithful saying that, "he who works little will gain little."

LESSON 7

bulb—ball-like root
fond—loving; adoring
tended—took care of; worked at
fragrance—scent; smell
pleasure—joy; delight
pretty—lovely; beautiful
bought—paid for; purchased
filled—packed; supplied
earth—ground; dirt
never—at no time
ever—at any time
produce—bear; bring forth
sprout—shoot of a plant
sprinkled—shook over
clapped—struck together
blooming—budding; blossoming
conduct—way one acts; behavior

The Bulb and the Flowers

Little Flora was very fond of flowers. She had many kinds of flowers in her garden, which she tended with great care. Their bright colors and sweet fragrance gave her much pleasure; but it made her feel sad when the frost came and killed her pretty flowers.

Her father bought a large vase, filled it with fine, soft earth, and gave her a bulb to plant in it. Flora had never seen flowers grow in a vase, and she did not think the bulb would ever produce flowers.

After a few days, the bulb began to swell in the vase, and a little green sprout was seen coming up.

"Oh! I am so happy," said Flora, "that the bulb bears flowers; for I can keep the vase in the house all winter."

One day, as she sprinkled water on the plant, she saw five little red buds among the leaves. Flora clapped her hands and said, "O Father! Come and see my plant; the buds are all blooming!"

Her father said, "All the blooms show how you have taken care of it; and your good conduct gives me as much pleasure as the flowers do you."

"Thank you, Father," said Flora. "If my conduct gives you as much pleasure as the flowers give me, you must be very happy."

LESSON 8

wise—smart; having understanding
world—earth
being—life; existence
guards—protects
harm—hurt; injury
thought—imagined; put into words
acts—actions; deeds
just—honest; upright
pure—clean; free from sin or guilt; holy
happy—joyful; delighted; blessed

God Made All Things

God is the Lord. He is great and wise and good.

He made us. He made all things.

He made the world. He made the sun and the

moon and the stars.

He made the land and the sea and the sky, and all things that are in them.

He made all the trees and plants that grow out of the earth, all the men and beasts that live on the land, all the birds that fly in the air, and all the fish that swim in the sea.

God is good, and does good at all times. He takes care of all things that He has made. If He did not take care of them and feed them, they would soon die and turn to dust.

God gave us our life and our breath. "In Him we live, and move, and have our being." (Acts 17:28).

He gives us the bread we eat and the clothes we wear. He guards us from harm all the day, and keeps us safe while we sleep in the night.

Though we cannot see the wind, yet it blows all around us, so God is with us at all times, though we see Him not.

There is no place where we can hide from God. If we had wings to fly to the ends of the earth, He would be there and know all we thought or said.

O, let us try, at all times, to do right! Let us speak no bad words, and do no bad acts.

Let us be kind, just, pure, and good; and then God will bless us, and we shall be happy.

LESSON 9

timid—nervous; fearful
burrow—a hole in the earth for animals
tender—soft; fragile
pinks—flowers of "pink" plants, such as
        carnations
parsley—plant used in cooking
twigs—small tree branches
shrubs—small bushes
hind—back (legs)
fore—front (legs)
depends—trusts; believes
reason—cause
slender—thin; not thick
bound—leap; spring
nimble—quick; fast
seldom—not often; hardly ever
creep—move without a sound
hunted—looked for
safety—guard; protection
raises—rears; lifts up
poet—writer of poetry

The Rabbit

The rabbit is a very shy and timid creature. In the daytime, it lies in its burrow; but, as soon as the night sets in, it comes out and hops around to look for food.

The rabbit feeds on tender herbs and plants. It is very fond of sweet apples, cabbage, turnips, clover, and green corn. Sometimes it will creep into the garden and nip the pinks and parsley. In the winter, when green herbs cannot be found, the rabbit feeds on buds, twigs, shrubs, and the bark of young trees.

The rabbit has large, round eyes; long ears; and long, slender legs. Its hind legs are much longer than its fore legs. For this reason, it can leap very far at a bound. The rabbit is very nimble; it can run so fast that even a fox or a dog can seldom catch it.

They are sometimes hunted for their flesh, which is thought, by many, to be very good food. Some say it tastes like chicken.

The rabbit cannot bite, like a dog, or scratch, like a cat; and for this reason, it is very timid. It depends on its long legs for safety. When it hears the least noise, it starts up, raises its long ears, and bounds away into the bushes, where it cannot be found.

Lesson 10

greedy—having an overly strong desire for something
healthy—well; in good shape
unripe—not ripe
for—because
obey—do as you are told; mind
became—came to be
ill—not well; sick
bear—put up with
assist—help; aid
conduct—the way one acts; behavior
realized—began to understand
careful—on the alert
self-control—strength of will; discipline
moderation—self-control; restraint

The Greedy Girl

Alice was eight years old. She was large for her age and enjoyed playing games. She could run and jump for hours at a time.

She was healthy and strong, and she might have been so for a long time, if she had been good and had done as she was told.

But Alice enjoyed cakes, pies, and candies; and, when she could get them, she would eat too much. She also liked to eat fruit that was not ripe.

Her mother had told her she must not eat unripe fruit; for, if she did, it would make her sick. But Alice did not obey her mother.

One day, Alice became very ill; and, for two weeks, she had to stay in her lonely bedroom. She had such a pain in her stomach that she could not bear to hear the children play or even the little birds sing.

When Alice began to get better, she was so weak that she could not stand or walk without someone to assist her. She could not run, jump, or play for a long time. She could not go into the fields with the other boys and girls or eat the ripe fruit.

But while she was ill and could not sleep most of the night, she thought a great deal about her past conduct. Alice realized that those who had told her not to eat too much were her best friends. She also realized that she had done wrong not to obey them.

When Alice became well again, she was careful about what she ate and tried to do as she was told. She grew to be a strong, healthy girl.

Many children need to learn the importance of self-control. Alice learned this lesson by understanding the value of controlling her eating habits. The Bible teaches all people—young and old—to do all things in moderation.

LESSON 11

carving—cutting in wood or stone
jackknife—large pocket-knife
noble—honorable; good
deeds—actions; works
respect—honor; praise
acquire—gain; get
secure—make safe; get hold of
esteem—high regard; admire
chosen—preferred; selected

Frank Carving His Name on a Tree

Rita: What is that boy trying to do with his jackknife, Mom?

Mother: He is trying to carve out the letters of his name on that tree.

Rita: Why is he carving his name on a tree?

Mother: I do not know, Rita. But the boy's name is Frank, and he is trying to make the letters of his name—F-R-A-N-K.

Rita: I do not think he is very smart, because he is carving letters on the bark of a tree. It might hurt the tree.

Mother: You are right; but, if he would work hard and learn well, his name may be known all over the world.

Rita: Will his name be read on that tree by more people than it would be if it were printed in a book?

Mother: No; but, if he learns to love God with all his heart, he will become a good man; and, if he does great and noble deeds, everyone will love and respect him.

Rita: Mom, I think I will try to get a good name by doing good and noble deeds.

Mother: That is the true way to acquire a good name—to trust and obey God and to secure the love and esteem of all good men. Remember, Rita, "A good name is rather to be chosen than great riches, ..." (Proverbs 22:1).

Lesson 12

darling—dearly beloved
seek—look for
amuse—make smile; please
strike—hit; beat
naughty—bad; disobedient
please—make happy; give pleasure to
listen—hear; pay attention
merry—happy; cheerful
tired—bored; uninterested

My Darling Brother

Little brother, darling boy,
You are very dear to me;
I am happy—full of joy,
When your smiling face I see.

How I wish that you could speak,
And could know the words I say!
Pretty stories I would seek,
To amuse you every day,

All about the honeybees,
Flying past us in the sun;
Birds that sing among the trees,
Lambs that in the meadows run.

I'll be very kind to you,
Never strike nor make you cry,
As some naughty children do;
But to please you I will try.

Shake your rattle—here it is,
Listen to its merry noise;
And, when you are tired of this,
I will bring you other toys.

Lesson 13

cheerful—happy; joyful
lively—active; full of life
arrange—set in order
teases—laughs at; makes fun of
playmates—friends in play
mistake—error; fault
comfort—cheer up; console
wishes—desires; needs
willful—stubborn; unruly
joins—unites
offend—hurt somebody's feelings; displease
injure—hurt; harm
evil—sin; wrongdoing
willing—ready; eager
behave—act; conduct oneself
manner—way of doing
praise—admire; honor
deserve—be worthy of; earn

The Kind Little Girl

Amy is a good girl. She is so kind and gentle that all who know her love her. All the little girls are glad when she comes to see them, for she tries to make them happy.

Amy is cheerful and lively, and is always ready to assist others who may need her help. She can show the girls how to dress their dolls and to arrange their little playthings.

She never teases any of her playmates when they make a mistake in speaking; and if anyone is sad,

Amy tries to comfort her.

If the girls begin some game, when she wishes to have some other, she is not angry or willful; but joins in the sport.

If her playmates offend her, she does not try to injure them, but tries to return good for evil.

When she is given anything nice, she is not selfish but is willing to share it with others.

Amy loves everyone, and tries to do good to all; and that is the reason why everyone loves her.

If all children would act like little Amy, and do unto others as they would have others do unto them, how much more happy they would be!

All children like to have others speak well of them. They should try, at all times, to behave in such a manner as to deserve the praise of others.

Little Amy also showed us the secret to gaining new friendships, for as the Bible states, "If a person is to have friends, he must show himself friendly" (Proverbs 18:24a).

LESSON 14

poultry—farm fowls; chickens, turkeys, etc.
gather—collect; bring together
cackling—making the noise of a hen
gabbling—making a confused noise
gobbling—making a noise of a turkey
noisy—loud; harsh sounds
tame—not wild; gentle
edge—rim, border
hencoop—cage for fowls (or hens)
crows—call of the rooster
spreads—makes bigger; extends
curves—bends; arcs
struts—walks with lofty steps; prances
share—part; portion
proudly—self-importantly; smugly
group—crowd; throng

Lucy Feeding the Poultry

Ah! What a lively time it is among the poultry!

Lucy has come out with a basket of corn on her arm to feed them.

When she calls, all the chickens, ducks, geese, and turkeys gather around her for their breakfast.

What a cackling, gabbling, and gobbling—all at the same time! It is their way of talking. They are like some noisy children, all talking at the same time.

How tame the pigeons are! One sits on the edge of the basket and picks up the corn, while another sits on Lucy's shoulder.

See the old rooster. It stands upon the hencoop and crows, while the hens and chickens are picking up the corn.

The turkey spreads out its tail, curves its neck, and struts about in a very proud manner. It walks around and looks on, until the rest get all they want, and then it comes to get its share.

The peacock, too, acts very proudly. It stands on a high box, as though it feels too proud to be seen with the rest of the group. When the peacock opens its large tail feathers, like a big fan, Lucy can enjoy all the lovely colors God gave this beautiful bird.

LESSON 15

named—gave name to
because—for the reason
fond—loving
follow—go after
hunt—seek; search
wreath—garland
blossom—flower
daisies—a kind of flower
buttercups—bright yellow flowers
prettier—more beautiful

Anna and Her Lamb

Anna had a pretty white lamb. Her aunt gave it to her, when the lamb was very young. Anna named her little lamb Snowball, because it was as white as snow.

She took good care of Snowball and fed it bread and milk every day. At night, she made a nice, warm bed of straw for it to lie on.

In a few days, Snowball grew so fond of Anna that the lamb would follow her all around the yard, just like a little dog.

Sometimes Anna would go and hide behind the bushes, and then call out, "Bo-peep."

Snowball would answer her by crying, "Baa," and then it would run all around the yard and hunt in the bushes until it found her.

One day Anna made a beautiful wreath of clover blossoms, daisies, and buttercups; she tied it around Snowball's neck. When the lamb jumped about and shook its head, she thought there never was a prettier pet than her little Snowball.

When Anna was tired of playing games, she would sit down on the grass, and Snowball would come and lie down by her, laying its head on her lap.

Snowball was very fond of Anna, for she was kind to her pretty white lamb. If you want your pets to love you in the same way, always treat them kindly by following the example of the Good Shepherd.

LESSON 16

tried—made an effort
amuse—keep busy; interest
quite—very; really
nearly—almost
leave—quit; depart from
quiet—silent; not noisy
disturb—upset; bother
trouble—problem; worry
errand—job; duty; chore
brought—fetched
present—gift
loveliest—most beautiful

The First Rose of Spring

David did not have little brothers or sisters to play with him. So he was always happy when his mother could find time to have fun with him.

His kind mother tried to amuse him in every way she could. She would show him how to draw pictures, to throw his ball, and to fly his kite. Sometimes, when he would get into his little wagon, she would pull him around on the sidewalk.

One day, his mother became quite ill, and she did not leave her room for nearly three weeks. David was very sorry that his mother was sick.

He tried to keep quiet and still, so he would not disturb her. David also tried not to cause his mother any trouble. Besides, he was ready to be sent on an errand when she needed his help.

David was very happy when his mother began to get well. Right away, he went into the garden and brought her a beautiful red rose. With all his heart, he said, "Mother, you shall have the first rose of spring."

His mother thanked him for the beautiful present, and told him that his good conduct gave her more pleasure than the loveliest flower.

Lesson 17

selfish—self-centered; thinking only of one's self
along—next to; beside; down
orchard—group of fruit trees
none—not one
kindhearted—caring; giving; thoughtful
share—divide
after—later in time; following
aunt—sister of a parent

The Selfish Boy and the Kindhearted Girl

One day, as Joseph was walking along the road, he met Mr. Preston, who was working in his apple orchard. Mr. Preston gave Joseph two apples—one for himself and the other to take home to his sister Lori. But on his way home, Joseph ate both apples that Mr. Preston had given him.

The next day, as Joseph and his sister were going by Mr. Preston's orchard, he asked Lori how she liked the apple he sent her.

"I did not eat any of your apples, sir," said Lori.

"Joseph," said Mr. Preston, "what did you do with the apple I sent to your sister?" Joseph hung his head, and said, "I ate it myself."

"That was very wrong, Joseph," said Mr. Preston. "I will now give your sister Lori two large apples, and you shall have none for your unkind conduct."

Then Mr. Preston began to tell them about a kindhearted girl named Sarah. If she had anything nice given to her, she would always share it with her little brothers and sisters.

Mr. Preston said, "One day, after Sarah came home from school, her mother told her she could go and see her aunt. It was a fine day in June when the cherries were ripe, so her aunt gave her a basketful to take home. Sarah did not eat the cherries herself, as some greedy girls would have done; but she took them all home and gave some of the largest ones to each of her brothers and sisters.

"Joseph, you should remember that your sister Lori is as fond of good things as you are. You should always be willing to share them with her. The Bible is right when it states, 'It is more blessed to give than to receive' (Acts 20:35)."

Lesson 18

struck—hit
raised—lifted
dropped—let fall
meant—intended
expect—look for
cruel—unkind
touched—moved; stirred
overcome—conquer

A Kiss for a Smack

George was nine years of age, and his sister Kate was seven. They were homeschooled and usually got along well together.

But one day, as they were playing in the yard, George became upset and smacked Kate hard on her head. Then Kate became angry and raised her hand to smack him back.

When Mother saw what Kate was about to do, she said, "Kate, it would be better for you to kiss your brother."

Kate dropped her hand and looked at her mother, as though she did not know what her mother meant. Kate thought that if her brother struck her, she had the right to strike him back.

Her mother looked kindly at her and said again, "Kate, you had better kiss your brother. See how angry he looks!"

When Kate saw how mad he really was, she threw her arms around his neck and kissed him.

George did not expect such a kind act in return for his cruel deed. His heart was touched, and tears filled his eyes.

Kate took a tissue and wiped away his tears. Then she tried to comfort him by saying, "Don't cry, George, you did not hurt me much."

But this only made him more ashamed, to think that his sister should treat him so kindly, when he had been so mean to her.

If Kate had struck George back, he would not have been so ashamed. But by kissing him, she made him feel sorry for his unkind and cruel conduct.

Mother told Kate, "When someone strikes you, or does anything to you that you think is wrong, give a kiss for a smack. In this way, you will 'overcome evil with good' (Romans 12:21)."

Lesson 19

carriage—cart with a seat

pony—small horse

kid—baby goat

harness—straps, bands, and other parts of gear used by an animal to pull a cart

collar—part of a harness that fits around an animal's neck

guide—lead; direct

mind—heed; regard

patient—forbearing

coaxed—persuaded; won over

patted—touched gently with the hand

pleased—liked

strange—odd; uncommon

activity—action; doings

Frank Riding in His Carriage

Frank had a nice carriage, but he did not have a pony to draw it. But Frank's father had a large goat that he had raised from a little kid. Father named it Ram, because the young goat liked to ram its head into everything and everybody.

His father said, "Frank, you could make a harness for Ram and teach it to draw the carriage."

So Frank went right to work and made a collar and harness to fit the goat. Then he took a long rope and placed it around the goat's head, so that he could guide it.

When Frank first put the harness on Ram, it began to rear up on its hind legs and push Frank with its horns. Frank did not mind, for he knew it would take some time before he could teach the goat to pull him in his carriage.

Frank was very patient with Ram. He coaxed and patted the goat kindly, leading it around the yard. After a few days, he could drive it where he pleased.

One day, Frank rode along the road in his carriage, as the goat pulled him. Beside them, Ram's little kid ran and jumped. The little kid acted as though it did not know what to think of this strange, new activity. It leaped around the big goat and then ran along by the side of the carriage.

When the little goat gets older, Frank will also teach it to pull him in his carriage. If he is wise, Frank will begin to teach it to pull his carriage, before it gets too old.

LESSON 20

churning—mixing; stirring up
pasture—land for grazing
together—as one; at the same time
command—give an order to
fetch—go and bring back; return with
plunge—jump; rush
finding—looking for; discovering
refused—said no; stopped
seemed—looked as if; appeared
deceived—misled; tricked
before—earlier; in the past
practice—do over and over again in order to
　　　learn
deceit—dishonesty; trickery

James and His Dog, Dash

Mr. Norton was a farmer, and he owned a large dog, named Dash. At night, Dash would watch his house. In the daytime, the dog would help with churning the cream and driving the cows to pasture with Mr. Norton's son James.

There was a large pond in the pasture, where James and Dash used to go and play together. James would take a stick and throw it, as far as he could, into the water and then command Dash to go and fetch it. Dash would plunge into the water, grab the stick in his mouth, and swim with it to the shore.

Sometimes James would throw a stone into the water and then command Dash to go and fetch it. Dash would again rush into the water and look around for the stone; but the dog would soon return without finding it.

But James could not trick Dash in this way more than two or three times. The next time he threw a stone into the water and told Dash to go and fetch it, the dog refused. It seemed to say, "No; you have deceived me before, and now I do not know when to believe you."

If you wish to have your pet obey, you must be careful not to deceive it. The practice of deceit is wrong, even in a joke. It may lead to a very unhappy end. Like Dash, your pet may learn not to trust you when you give it a command.

Lesson 21

many—large number
remember—call to mind
picking—pulling off; plucking
command—give an order to
applies to—has to do with; refers to
else—also; as well; beside
whether—which of the two
gravel walk—walk covered with gravel
disappointed—upset; let down

"Thou Shalt Not Steal"

Ashley: Mother, may I go into Mr. Carey's garden today?

Mother: Why do you wish to go into his garden, Ashley?

Ashley: Because he has so many pretty flowers there, and I want to look at them closely.

Mother: Yes, Ashley; you may go, if you will only look at the flowers and not disturb them.

Ashley: What does disturb mean, Mother? Does it mean touch or take?

Mother: It means both. If you touch a flower, you disturb it; and no one can take a flower without disturbing it.

Ashley: Mother, why may I not take one rose, or one small flower? Mr. Carey has a great many flowers, and I am sure he will not miss one or two.

Mother: Do you remember the Bible lesson you learned last week?

Ashley: Yes; it was, "Thou shalt not steal." But it did not say anything about picking a rose.

Mother: True; but the command applies to a rose, as well as to anything else. It does not matter whether it is a small thing, or a big thing.

Ashley: Mother, if you will let me go today, I will not disturb any of the flowers.

Mother: Well, Ashley, put on your sweater, and you may go; but you must return by five o'clock.

＊＊＊＊＊

Ashley: O, Mother! See what a beautiful rose Mr. Carey gave me! I went along the gravel walk and did not touch one flower. He picked it himself and gave it to me. He is very kind.

Mother: I hope you learned that it is much better to obey God's Word by not stealing. If Mr. Carey had seen you take one or two of his flowers without asking, he would have been very angry and disappointed with you. Most likely, he would not have given you that beautiful rose.

Little Things

Little drops of water,
Little grains of sand
Make the mighty ocean,
And the pleasant land.

Thus the little minutes,
Humble though they be,
Make the mighty ages
Of eternity.

Thus our little errors
Lead the soul away
From the path of virtue,
Oft in sin to stray.

Little deeds of kindness,
Little words of love,
Make our earth an Eden,
Like the Heaven above.

LESSON 23

let's—let us
finished—completed
accidentally—by mistake
tumbled—fell
knocked—broken; ruined
harsh—hard; rude
intend—mean; design
quiver—shake; tremble
trivial—small; unimportant
admit—own; confess
fault—error; mistake
console—cheer up; comfort
hoped—wished; desired
forgive—let off; pardon

The Loving Children

Dennis and his little sister, Debbie, were very fond of each other; they were never happier than when they were playing with each other. Dennis always tried to amuse her, in every way he could.

Dennis would pull Debbie in his little red wagon all around the yard. Sometimes she would get up on the couch and put her arms around Dennis's neck, and he would give her a horseback ride. Debbie also liked to look at the pictures in their beautiful books, while Dennis would read to her a story.

One day Dennis said to his sister, "Let's make a house with our blocks, with doors and windows."

"Oh, that will be nice!" said Debbie. "I will help you bring the blocks, and we can build the house together."

When they had nearly finished, Debbie tried to place a block on top of the house for a chimney; but she accidentally hit her foot against the house and it tumbled down on the floor.

"Oh, Debbie!" yelled Dennis, in an angry tone of voice. "You have knocked the house down! I wish you would not play with me! You are always ruining things."

Debbie turned away in tears. Dennis had hurt her feelings. It was hard for Debbie to think that her dear brother, who had always been so kind, would speak to her in such a harsh way. After all, she did not intend to knock down the house.

When Dennis saw her lips and chin quiver and her big blue eyes fill with tears, he knew at once that he had done wrong to upset his sister for so trivial a matter.

His mother told him it was not right to blame his little sister, when she did not mean it. She told him to admit his fault and try to console her.

Dennis ran and threw his arms around Debbie's neck. He told her he was sorry for what he had said and hoped she would forgive him. Dennis wiped the tears from her face, and Debbie went back to playing with him, as happy as ever.

Children should be careful not to say or do anything that will hurt the feelings of their playmates; and when they have done wrong, like Dennis, they should confess their faults. Wise and godly children should always be slow to get angry. (Read James 1:19.)

LESSON 24

begged—asked for wholeheartedly; pleaded
nodded—move head up and down
rambled—roved; wandered
promised—gave his word; assured
beast—animal
searched—looked carefully
reply—answer; response
neighbors—persons living near
concerned—worried; troubled
feared—were afraid
precious—beloved; dear

Lost Children

"Mother," asked Henry, "will you please tell Laura and I a story?"

"You should say, 'Laura and me,'" corrected Mother.

"Will you tell Laura and me a story? Please!" begged Henry.

"Yes," said mother, "I will tell you a story about two children who were lost in the woods.

"One day, a little boy and girl went into the woods to pick some berries. Their names were Henry and Laura, and they were about as old as you two."

"Mom, were their names the same as ours?" asked Laura.

Mother nodded and went on, "After filling their baskets with berries, they started to go home, but they could not find their way. They rambled around in the woods until they were lost; they did not know which way to go.

"Laura had torn her dress, and spilled all her berries. She sat down and began to cry. Henry wiped the tears from her cheeks and told her not to cry; he promised to give her some of his berries.

"When night came on, the children had no supper and no place to sleep. So they ate the berries that Henry had picked. Then they lay down by the side of a large tree; but they could not sleep.

"They were afraid that some wild beast might kill them, and that they would never see their father and mother again.

"Since the children did not come home, when it began to get dark, their father and mother went to look for them. They searched for a long time in the woods, calling out 'Henry! Laura!'; but they did not hear a reply.

"Their parents then asked the neighbors if they had seen their children; but no one knew anything about them. Now their father and mother were very concerned, for they feared that their precious children were lost in the woods.

"First they called their pastor to pray for Henry and Laura and that God would help the parents find their children, safe and sound.

"Next the parents asked their neighbors to help them search for the children. Right away, their kind neighbors took their dogs, guns, and flashlights and started out to find Henry and Laura. They searched nearly all night without finding them.

"Then early in the morning, the parents heard the sound of a gun and prayed their children were found. Soon they saw one of the neighbors coming out of the woods, leading Henry and Laura by the hand.

"Oh, what joy filled the hearts of the father and mother, as they hugged their dear children! Then they all thanked God for protecting Henry and Laura and helping the search party to find them."

LESSON 25

central—middle
planned—laid out; designed
pleasant—agreeable
visit—go or come to see
planted—set out
shrubs—small bushes
different—not the same; unlike
uneven—not flat; not level
valleys—low lands between hills
making— forming; creating
skating—sliding on skates
weather—state of the air
sailing—moving, like a vessel
grand—great; wonderful
slender—slim; small
vessel—boat; ship
tame—not wild; gentle
down—fine feathers

Central Park

In the city of New York, there is a very large park, called Central Park. This park has been planned with great care, so as to make it a pleasant place for people to visit.

The rocks, in many places, have been cut away, and the grounds have been planted with shrubs and trees. The grounds also have very fine roads and walkways, leading in different directions so that people can ride or walk to any part they wish.

The park is quite uneven, being made up of many little hills and valleys. Some of the little valleys have been filled with water, making a number of lakes or ponds.

In winter, when these ponds are frozen over, the boys and girls have a wonderful time skating. When the weather is pleasant and the skating is good, you may see thousands of people, of almost all ages, skating at the same time.

In the summertime, you may see a number of large white swans, sailing around on the water. It is a grand sight to see them curve their long, slender necks, and float around on the water. They spread out their large wings, like the sails of a vessel, and the wind blows them along. They are so tame that they will come and eat corn or crumbs of bread from your hand.

The girl in the picture is feeding one of these large white swans. There are also two young swans by her side. They have very fine, soft down, which they will keep until they get to be five or six months old. Do you know what these young swans are called? They are called cygnets.

Lesson 26

goslings—young geese
thrashing—beating; spanking
purpose—reason; goal
won't—will not
flock—group of animals
suppose—think; imagine
desire—want; longing
temper—calmness of mind
conquer—overcome

Jeff Learns a Lesson

Jeff lived on a farm with his family. They had many animals to care for, such as cows, pigs, chickens, and geese.

Jeff was very fond of pets; he always wanted to have some kind of animal with which to play. At different times, he had a kitten or a puppy or a rabbit for a pet.

One day Jeff saw some little goslings swimming in a brook near his house, and he thought he would take one home and make it his pet.

But as soon as he picked one up in his hands, its mother flew at Jeff and gave him such a thrashing with its wings that he dropped it and ran into the house.

A few days later, Jeff's mother wanted to pick the feathers off the older geese, so she put them into the barn for that purpose; but she left the little goslings in the yard by themselves.

When Jeff saw that the older geese were shut up, where they could not harm him, he took a stick and killed one of the goslings.

When his mother learned what he had done, she asked, "Why, Jeff? Why did you kill one of my precious little goslings?"

"Because," argued Jeff, "a mother goose gave me a beating, when I tried to take one of her goslings home."

"Yes; but the little gosling is not to blame for what its mother did," Jeff's mother said firmly.

But Jeff asked, "Won't the goslings grow up and become geese if I don't kill them?"

"Of course they will, my son," said Jeff's mother. "Someday they will make a fine flock of geese."

"Well, then," questioned Jeff, "won't they be just as mean as their mother and beat me when I go near them?"

"I suppose they will," said his mother, "if you try to steal away one of their goslings again."

"Well, that is the reason why I started to kill them now!" said Jeff, "so they won't grow up to be geese and attack me."

"You forget, my dear son," said his mother, "that God Himself gave all mothers the natural desire to protect their little babies. You should never fault a mother for doing her job well. I trust that you would want your mother to protect you, if you were attacked someday. Is that not true?"

"Well, I think so," said Jeff, "but what can I do to make things right again?"

"Ask God to forgive you for killing one of His creatures, when you foolishly lost your temper," said Jeff's mother. "Ask Him also for the strength to conquer your hot temper."

"Is that all I need to do, Mother?" asked Jeff.

"Yes, my son," said his mother, "if you are truly sorry for what you did, God will forgive you and help you to do what is right."

LESSON 27

assists—helps out; aids
active—lively; energetic
eager—ready; willing
errand—task; job
winding—wrap around
needed—wanted
neatly—nicely; well

Colin Assists His Mother

Colin was an active boy. He was always busy doing something useful, either for himself or his loving parents.

During his home school classes, he was always

eager to complete his lessons and loved reading books. He also enjoyed working around the house.

Colin, like other boys, was fond of play. But when his mother asked him to go on an errand for her, he would stop playing, at once, and do what he was told. In this, he was not like other boys who, when asked to do any thing, would say, "Wait until I am done playing; then I will do it."

One morning, as Colin was going out with his slingshot, his mother asked him to assist her in winding some yarn. He put away his slingshot, went into the house, and held the coil of yarn on his hands, while his mother wound it.

While Colin was helping his mother, he asked, "What are you going to do with the ball of yarn?"

She answered, "I am going to knit you a pair of socks, and you may have what is left to make a ball."

"Thank you, Mother," said Colin, "but what should I use for a cover?"

"I will give you some money, and you can take the ball of yarn to the shoemaker, and he will cover it for you," said his mother.

When Colin's mother had used all the yarn she needed to knit his socks, there was a large ball left.

Colin took the ball of yarn to the shoemaker, who covered it neatly with a piece of soft leather.

Colin took out his money to pay him; but the shoemaker said, "Keep your money, my boy. I only hope I have done you some good."

"Thank you, sir," said Colin. "I did not expect you to cover the ball for free. If I can be of any service to you, I shall be most happy to help you out."

"You are welcome," said the shoemaker, smiling.

It was the gentle and quiet spirit that Colin had as a boy, which helped him to become an honorable man.

Lesson 28

chimney sweep—someone who cleans soot
from inside a chimney
ago—past; gone
free—open to all
astonished—surprised; amazed
showing—pointing out
over—above
plenty—more than enough; abundance
instruct—teach, educate

The Little Chimney Sweep

Some years ago, a group of Christian men in Chicago provided a free school for all the little chimney sweeps, so they could learn to read.

One day, a teacher at the school asked one of the sweeps if he knew his letters.

"Yes, sir!" said the boy. "I know them all."

"Do you know how to read and spell?" asked the teacher.

"Yes, sir," answered the lad. "I learned to read and spell, some time ago."

"What book did you learn to read from?" the teacher asked.

"Oh, I never had any book!" said the little sweep.

"Will you tell me, then," asked the teacher, "how you learned to read and spell?"

"Another sweep, who was a little older than I

am, taught me," answered the boy.

The astonished teacher asked, "How could he do it, without a book?"

"He did it by showing me the letters on the signs over the shop doors," said the sweep. "We read them as we went through the city."

The only teacher this little boy had was a sweep, like himself; and his only books were the signs over the doors of the shops and stores.

If this poor little sweep—who never had been to school—could learn to read without the help of books, how much more should children learn, who have plenty of good books to read and good teachers to instruct them!

Lesson 29

brightest—most brilliant
hues—shades of color
crowned—invested with a crown
weave—lace together; knit
prettiest—most beautiful
wreath—headdress; circlet
brow—forehead
twig—shoot or branch of a tree
shape—form
manner—way; fashion
placed—put; set
declared—stated; announced
fade—lose color
highly—greatly
prize—value

The May Queen

One fine spring day, Robert and his two sisters, Clara and Darla, went out into the woods to gather flowers. They soon filled their basket with buds and blossoms of the brightest hues—red, white, blue, purple, yellow, and orange.

"Now," said Robert, "which of you will be crowned 'May Queen,' Clara or Darla?"

"Oh," said Clara, "let us weave the prettiest flowers into a wreath and place it on the brow of our mother. We will make her our May Queen!"

"Good!" said Robert. "That will make her so happy, because she is very fond of wildflowers."

Then Robert cut a small twig and bent it in the shape of a hoop. Next, Clara and Darla tied the flowers around it. In this manner, they made a beautiful wreath.

After that, they took the wreath home, and Clara and Darla placed it on their mother's head. They declared, "You are our May Queen."

Then Robert gave the rest of the flowers in his basket to his mother. She put them into a pitcher of water and placed them on the table, where they soon filled the room with a sweet smell.

Their mother was pleased and said, "Though the flowers will soon fade, yet I highly prize this gift, because it has been given by my own loving children."

LESSON 30

easily—with no trouble
receive—get; obtain
perfect—complete; without error
fail—fall short; miss
won—gained
justly—honestly; fairly
merited—earned; deserved
gilt— gold-painted
edges—borders
concordance—alphabetical list of words
     from the Bible and references where
     they occur in the Bible
references—places where words from the
     Bible occur—book of the Bible, chap-
     ter, and verse

Joelle's Present

Joelle was a very good girl, but she could not learn her Sunday school lessons as easily as some of the girls in her class.

One time, she told her mother that her Sunday school teacher was going to give a Bible as a present to the girl who would receive the most marks for perfect lessons and good conduct.

"But there is no use trying to get it," Joelle said sadly, "because Emma can learn much faster than I can. I am sure she will get it."

"If you try as hard as Emma does, do you think you can learn your lessons as well as she?" asked her mother.

"I do not know," said Joelle. "But, if I cannot learn as fast as she does, I can at least try to behave as well."

"That, I think, will please your teacher just as much as getting perfect lessons," said her mother. "Yet I do not think you will fail them, if you get up early in the morning and study hard."

"Well, Mother, I am willing to try," said Joelle, "if you will listen to me practice my lessons, before I go each Sunday."

From the next Sunday until the end of the year, the teacher marked Joelle's lessons and conduct perfect; and so she won the prize.

All the girls in the class seemed glad that Joelle

received the present, because they all said she had justly merited it.

The present was a large, beautiful Bible, with a bright red cover and gilt edges. It had full-color maps and a concordance, filled with words from the Bible and where they could be found.

* * * * *

If you think you cannot learn as fast as others, or behave as well, then you should try to do as Joelle did. Like her, you may become the best student in your class, or even in the Sunday school. It is a wise saying that "practice makes perfect."

Copy and memorize the following poem:

> If a task is once begun,
> Never leave it till it's done;
> Be the labor great or small,
> Do it well or not at all.

LESSON 31

rover—rambler
nimblest—quickest
fleet—swift
honest—truthful; sincere
moment—instant; second
across—over; to the other side
loudly—noisily
sport—play
plain—level land
chase—run after; pursue
in vain—for nothing; without hope
plat—small piece of ground
abroad—not at home
where'er—at whatever place

The Boy and His Dog Rover

Old Rover is the nimblest
That ever ran a race;
His ear so quick, his foot so fleet,
And such an honest face.

My playmate he, in every sport,
The moment I begin:
He's always ready for a race,
And always sure to win.

One day, he stole my hat, and ran
Away across the plain;
While loudly laughed a boy and man
Who saw me chase in vain.

So, tired at last, I sat me down
Upon a green grass-plat,
When quick, old Rover turned about,
And brought me back my hat.

At home, abroad, where'er I go,
There Rover's sure to be;
There never was a kinder dog,
Than he has been to me.

Lesson 32

truth teller—one who tells the truth
tossing—throwing upward
owner—one who owns something
wicked—sinful; evil
intending—planning; having in mind
showing—letting (somebody) see; presenting
praised—spoke well of; honored
toward—in the direction of
indeed—in truth
devious—dishonest; lying
be rewarded—be paid back; gain something
proves—makes certain

The Truth Teller

As a little boy was tossing a penny into the air, it fell over a big fence and into a garden. He tried to climb over the fence and get it. But when he found he could not do so, he sat down on the ground and cried.

The owner of the garden, hearing the noise, looked over the fence and asked the little boy, "Why are you crying?"

"I have lost a piece of money," said the boy, "which a good man gave me for taking a kitten from some wicked boys, who were going to kill it."

The man took a large piece of money out of his pocket and said to the boy, "Is this the piece of money you lost?"

"No, sir," said the boy, for he would not have

told a lie for a great many pieces of gold. "The piece that I lost was not gold."

"Was it this, then?" said the man, showing him a silver half-dollar.

"No, sir," said the truthful boy; "it was not silver."

"Is it this?" said the man, showing him the penny he had lost.

"Oh yes!" said the lad. "That is the very piece. I know it by the little hole in it; for I was intending to put a string through the hole, and hang the penny on my little sister's neck."

The man said, "You are such a good boy, I will give you the gold and silver coins that I showed you, as well as your own penny."

The little boy was very happy that he had told the truth. He thanked the man and ran to tell his playmates about how this kind man had blest him.

Everyone loved this little boy and praised him because he told the truth and would not tell a lie— even to get money.

Another boy, who saw this good little boy's money and heard him tell how he got it, thought he would try to get some money from this kind man in the same way.

He ran toward the garden, which was a few blocks away. When he came near the fence, he threw over a penny. Then he sat down and began to cry very loudly.

The man came to him and asked him why he was crying.

"I have lost some money," said the dishonest boy, "which my father gave me to buy some bread with, and he will beat me when I go home."

"Is this the money you lost?" said the good man, showing him a piece of gold.

"Yes, sir," said the boy; "that is the very piece."

"Indeed, it is not," said the man; "and for telling a lie, you shall not have this money; but here is your own."

This devious boy thought he would be rewarded by telling a lie; but the conduct of the good boy proves that God always honors those who speak the truth.

LESSON 33

measure—work out; compute
aid—help; assistance
equal—the same
task—job; activity
distance—length; space
between—put in the middle
figure—number
strikes—beats; hits
o'clock—of the clock
proper—just; correct
forever—without end; eternally

How Time Is Measured

Clocks and watches are used to measure time. It would be a hard task to measure time without the aid of clocks or watches.

On the face of the clock there are twelve numbers that are placed at equal distances from each other. Between each of these numbers are four small dots, as well as one dot by each of the numbers; they all add up to sixty dots. Each dot stands for one of the sixty minutes in an hour.

The long hand moves from one figure to another in five minutes, and it moves from 12 to 12 in one hour. The long hand is called the minute hand.

The short hand moves from one number to another in sixty minutes. So, it takes the short hand twelve hours to move all around the face of the clock. The short hand is called the hour hand.

When the hour hand points to 1, and the minute hand points to 12, the clock strikes one; it is one o'clock.

When the hour hand points to 2, and the minute hand points to 12, the clock strikes two; it is two o'clock.

When the hour and minute hands both point to 12, the clock strikes twelve times, and it is then twelve o'clock.

Sixty seconds make one minute; sixty minutes

make one hour; twenty-four hours make one day; seven days make one week; four weeks make one month; twelve months make one year.

We should be careful to make a proper use of time, as it passes; for, time once passed never returns. The moment that is lost is lost forever. God, our Creator, expects us to make good use of our time (John 9:4; Ephesians 5:15, 16).

LESSON 34

appear—are seen
turtle—species of dove
groves—clusters of trees
robbed—cheated; deprived
beauty—loveliness
merely—only
looked upon—thought about; considered
thieves—robbers
sowed—scattered (as grain); planted
reaped—gathered
scolded—warned about; corrected
twittered—chirped
destroyed—ruined; damaged
crops—grain, fruit, etc.
army—number; throng
save—keep safe; protect
havoc—mess; destruction

The Helpful Birds

"For, lo, the winter is past, the rain is over and gone. The flowers appear on the earth; the time of the singing of birds is come, and the voice of the turtle [dove] is heard in our land." (Song of Solomon, 2:11, 12)

Welcome to the birds! They make springtime cheerful. Their glad notes are heard in the fields, gardens, and groves. Even springtime would be robbed of much of its beauty and pleasure were it not for the sweet music of the birds.

But God did not create birds merely to please our eyes and our ears. He made them to help care for the grain and the fruit that the farmers grow.

Blackbirds were once looked upon as great thieves. Farmers thought these birds took more than their share of the oats, rye, and corn. The farmers sowed; and, so it was said, the blackbirds reaped. The farmers scolded, and the birds twittered. The farmers drove the birds away from their fields, but they soon came back again.

Indeed, the blackbirds were not after the farmers' grain at all; they were after the worms, which would have destroyed their crops. So, the next year the blackbirds did not visit the fields, and the crops were nearly destroyed by a great army of worms.

What could the farmers do? Who could help save their crops? Who could help but their best friends—the blackbirds?

At last, the blackbirds came to the farmers' aid and made a great havoc among the worms; therefore, the farmers' grain was saved. After that, the farmers welcomed the blackbirds to their fields, because they always cared for the grain.

Lesson 35

living—income; livelihood
spare—do without; afford
lent—let (somebody) use; loaned
profit—gain; benefit
thus—therefore; as a result
selling—give (something) for money
besides—in addition to
earning—gaining (money or wages) by labor
rare—not common; hardly ever seen
piece—coin; portion of money
mistake—error; slip-up
really—in truth
effort—energy; willpower
stranger—unknown person
correct—make right; fix
belong—fit in; appertain
alley—narrow back street; lane
clerk—writer or assistant
gentleman—well brought-up man
partner—joint owner
business—one's work
dealings—tradings

The Oranges Jordan Sold

Jordan was a young boy, who sold oranges in the street for a living. Jordan's father was dead, and his mother was very poor. She had to work hard to get food for herself and four small children.

Jordan, who was the oldest, said he could help her, if he only had a little money to buy some oranges. His mother gave him what little she could spare, and he went and bought a basketful. Then he sold the oranges for twice as much as he paid for them.

Jordan gave back to his mother the money she lent him; and, with the profit, he bought another basket of oranges.

Thus he went on, buying and selling oranges. In this way, he helped his poor mother, besides earning his own living.

One day, a man bought some oranges from Jordan; and, in paying for them, gave Jordan a rare five-dollar gold piece by mistake. Jordan put the money into his pocket without counting it.

Soon after the man had gone, Jordan began to count the money he received. When he saw the five-dollar gold piece, he took up his basket of oranges and ran to find the man who had given it to him.

He soon found the man and said, "Sir, I think you made a mistake when you paid for the oranges."

"How so?" asked the man. "Did I not pay the full price?"

"Yes, sir," said Jordan. "But, with the payment, you gave this rare five-dollar gold piece. It must be worth a lot more money than five dollars!"

"A gold piece!" said the man, as he put his hand into his pocket, to find out if it was really so.

"Ah, yes! You are right, my boy," said the man. "But why did you take so much effort to run after a stranger, to correct his mistake?"

"Because," said Jordan, "I have been taught to be honest and never to take anything that does not belong to me."

"You are an honest boy," said the man. "And

now, I should like to know your name and where you live."

"My name is Jordan; and I live with my mother in that small house, by the alley," pointed the boy.

The next day, the man sent a large basketful of nice, sweet oranges to Jordan as a present.

When Jordan was sixteen years of age, the man sent for him to come and serve him as a clerk in his store. So Jordan went to live with the gentleman; and, after a few years, he became a partner in his business.

Jordan was honest in all his dealings, and soon he became a very rich man. This shows that, if you are always honest, God will bless you.

Lesson 36

uncle—brother of a parent
watched—looked closely
appeared—came into view
laden—filled; weighed down
hardly—only just; barely
arrived—got there; pulled in
aunt—sister of a parent
cousins—children of an aunt and uncle
greeted—said "hello" to; saluted
brood—group; family
delighted—pleased; happy
frightened—scared
snug—cozy; warm
pantry—closet
covered—spread over
insects—bugs; creatures
pasture—field; grazing land

Amanda's Visit to the Country

Amanda lived in the city, and she had an uncle who lived in the country; he was a farmer. Amanda liked to run in his fields and pick buttercups and clover blossoms.

In spring, Amanda watched to see when the grass in the yard would turn green. When the very first dandelion appeared, she ran to her mother and said, "The 'sunshine' has now come; when shall we go to see Uncle Phil?"

In July she had her wish. As she rode along, she saw the trees laden with fruit and the gardens filled with flowers. She was in such a hurry to get to Uncle Phil's farm that she could hardly sit in the car.

At last, they arrived at her uncle's place. Her aunt and her little cousins were all glad to see Amanda and her mother.

As soon as she greeted her aunt and uncle, she ran out to the barn with her cousins to see the cow and the calf. She also saw the white hen, which had a fine brood of chickens; and Amanda was delighted when she first saw them running about to pick up the seeds.

After drinking some cold lemonade, all the children went into the fields to gather flowers. On the way, Amanda saw a little squirrel run along the top of a stone wall. She wanted to take it home to live with her in the city; so she ran after it, thinking she could catch it. But the squirrel hid itself, where Amanda could not find it.

Her mother told her she was glad Amanda did not catch the squirrel, because, if she had taken hold of it, it would have been frightened and might have bitten her.

Upon hearing this, Amanda said she did not want the squirrel; but she did ask her mother to tell about its snug house and little pantry, full of nuts.

In the evening, Amanda saw some fireflies; and she said to her uncle, "See how the ground is covered with pretty little stars! Did they come from the sky?"

Her uncle told her they were insects; and that God made them so that they could give light from their bodies.

Then Amanda asked her uncle to tell her their name. He said the people in the country called them "lightning bugs."

Amanda had never seen fireflies before and talked a great deal about them. But, when she tried to tell her mother about them, she forgot their name and said, "O Mother! I have seen some 'thunder bugs'!"

The next day, Amanda went into the meadow with her cousins to pick some cranberries. She had never seen berries like these before, so she called them "little red apples"—just big enough for her doll.

As the children were coming home, they heard a great noise behind the barn, and they all ran to see what it was. There, in the pasture, was an angry dog that was growling and trying to bite a poor little calf.

But a great ox was also in the pasture, and it ran to the calf to protect it. When the dog tried to bite the calf, the ox would charge at the dog with its horns. At last, the dog was driven off, and the calf was not hurt.

Amanda called the ox a "good cow," and wanted to give it some of the cranberries in her little basket. But her cousins told her the ox was not that friendly.

When it was time for Amanda to go home to the city, she cried. But her mother told her how much her father wanted to see his little girl, and how he would like to hear about the things she had seen in the country. Amanda loved her father, so she stopped crying and began to pack her things.

When Amanda returned home, she told her father all about the chickens, the squirrel, the ox, and the fireflies—and what a mistake she made in calling them "thunder bugs."

Lesson 37

difficult—hard to be done
task—job; chore
pattern—model; example
expects—desires; looks for
attempt—try; effort
almost—nearly
perform—do; accomplish
skill—great ability
labor—work
enables—gives power
worth—value; importance

The Difficult Task

Andrew: Father, my art teacher wants me to draw the branch of a rosebush, with one rose on it; but I cannot do it.

Father: My son, I do not think your teacher would ask you to do anything you are not able to do.

Andrew: Well, I have tried and tried to draw it; but it does not look at all like the pattern. I wish you would draw it for me.

Father: Do you think it would be right for me to draw your picture, when your teacher expects you to do it?

Andrew: No, sir; but I can never draw that rose, like the one in the picture. I know I cannot.

Father: Try again; it may not be as difficult as you now think it is. Give it one more attempt, and then let me see it.

✳ ✳ ✳ ✳ ✳

Andrew: Father, I have done it! I have done it! It now looks almost as good as the pattern.

Father: Yes, Andrew; you have done very well.

Aren't you glad that I did not draw the picture for you?

Andrew: Yes, Father; and now I think I will be able to draw another picture much better than this one.

Father: Yes; every task you perform by your own skill and labor enables you to perform still greater ones. Remember, my son, that anything that does not cost you time, thought, or labor is not worth very much.

LESSON 38

delight—great pleasure
skip—leap; bound
merrily—happily; cheerfully
primrose—early rose
extend—spread; expand
painted—colored
leaping—jumping
lark—type of bird
mounts—ascends
scarce—hardly
sure—certain
rook—type of crow

The Spring Time

I'm very glad the spring is come;
The sun shines out so bright;
The little birds upon the trees,
Are singing with delight.

The young grass looks so fresh and green,
The lambs do sport and play;
And I can skip and run about,
As merrily as they.

I like to see the daisies blue,
And buttercups once more,
The primrose, and the rosebush too,
And every pretty flower.

I like to see the butterfly
Extend her painted wing;
And all things seem just like myself,
So pleased to see the spring.

The fishes in the little brook
Are leaping up so high;
The lark is singing very sweet,
And mounts into the sky;

The rooks are building up their nests
Upon the large oak tree;
And everything's as full of joy,
As ever it can be.

There's not a cloud upon the sky,
There's nothing dark or sad:
I jump, and scarce know what to do,
I feel so very glad.

God must be very good indeed,
Who made each pretty thing;
I'm sure I ought to love Him much,
For bringing back the spring.

Lesson 39

silly—foolish
shepherd—person who takes care of sheep
nursed—looked after; tended
climbed—went up; ascended
steep—high; sheer
fold—sheep pen
contented—happy; satisfied
slyly—secretly
hedge—row of bushes
frisk—romp and play
glee—joy; delight
den—cave of a wild animal
carried—held while moving; conveyed
trouble—difficulty
regret—be sorry
authority—charge; responsibility

The Silly Lamb

There was once a good shepherd who had a great many sheep and lambs, for which he cared. He always led them by clean water to drink and fresh grass to eat.

If any of them became ill, he nursed them back to health. Also, when they climbed up steep hills and the lambs became tired, he would carry them in his arms.

Every night the shepherd drove the sheep and lambs into the fold, where they lay snug and warm. Moreover, the shepherd's dog lay outside the fold, to guard them from wild beasts.

They were all contented with the kind care of the shepherd, except one foolish little lamb that did not like to be shut up. This silly lamb seemed to think, if it could run and skip about by moonlight and go where it pleased, it would be much more happy than it would to be shut up in the fold, with the rest of the flock.

One evening, when the shepherd called the sheep to come into the fold, this foolish little lamb would not obey. It crept slyly under a hedge and hid itself.

When the rest of the sheep and lambs were in the fold, fast asleep, the foolish lamb came out to run, skip, and frisk about in glee. After that, it jumped over a small fence and ran into the woods.

But soon, a large wolf came out of its den and gave a very fierce growl. At once the silly lamb wished it had been shut up in the fold; but that was a long way off, and the lamb did not know how to get back to it. In the end, the wolf seized the poor lamb, carried it off to its dark den, and ate it up.

Boys and girls who wish to have their own way, like this silly lamb, will most likely get into trouble. If so, they will surely regret that they did not obey those whom God has put in authority over them (Ephesians 6:1–3).

Lesson 40

supplies—gives; provides
fattened—made fat or fleshy
tallow—hard animal fat
hide—skin of an animal
tanned—changed into leather
obtain—get a hold of; receive
rocky—stony; covered with rocks
branches—tree limbs; boughs
withered—dried up; shrunken
trunk—body of tree
pierced—poked a hole in
yields—brings into being; produces
freely—without limit; plentifully
native—belonging to a country by birth
grateful—thankful
goodness—kindness; uprightness

The Milk Givers

The cow is one of the most useful animals. It supplies us with milk, cream, butter, and cheese. When it is well fattened, its flesh is good for food, and its tallow is made into wax paper, crayons, and soap. When its hide is tanned, it makes thick, strong leather. Out of this leather, we often make boots and coats.

But cows are not the only milk givers. In South America, people obtain very rich milk from a tree, called the "Cow Tree." The Cow Tree grows on dry, rocky land, where there is no grass and where the cow could find no pasture.

The Cow Tree's branches and leaves look withered; but when its trunk is pierced, rich milk flows from it. The tree yields most freely in the early morning. Then the native people may be seen around it, with their pitchers, obtaining its rich milk.

How good and wise is God, who provides for the needs of all His creatures! Let us be grateful for His goodness, and serve Him with all our heart, mind, and strength.

Lesson 41

order—direct
excited—keyed up; eager
immediately—right away; at once
anxious—eager; concerned
spade—small shovel
spread—put on; scatter
flowerbed—bed of flowers; piece of ground
attempt—try to do
perform—able to do; carry out
wheeled—rolled
discovered—found out; learned
benefit—advantage
blessing—God's goodness

Gavin's Wheelbarrow

Most of all Gavin wanted to have a new wheelbarrow to help in the garden. Since he had been such a good boy, his father told him he could go to the store and order one. Gavin was so excited that he set off immediately.

When Gavin arrived, the man at the store was very busy and could not order it just then, so Gavin had to wait several minutes. He was so anxious that he could hardly wait. After a short time, the man ordered a nice, big wheelbarrow. But Gavin had to wait again until it was sent to his home.

Two weeks later, a large box was delivered to Gavin's home. His wheelbarrow had arrived! It was a very nice-looking one, indeed. The wheelbarrow was painted bright red—inside and out; the handles were white, and the wheel was black.

Gavin rolled his new wheelbarrow into the garden and asked his father to give him some work to do. His father told him he could take his spade, put some dirt into his wheelbarrow, and spread the dirt on the flowerbed.

Gavin did as he was told, but he filled his wheelbarrow so full that he could not move it. Then his father said, "Son, you must take out some of the dirt, and then you will be able to roll it."

After Gavin removed some of the dirt, he found he could roll it along very easily. This taught him never to attempt more than he could perform. So he wheeled the dirt to the flowerbed and turned the wheelbarrow on its side, spilling the dirt out.

Gavin worked hard until he became tired and hungry. He was so glad when his mother called him to dinner. He told her, "I like my wheelbarrow very much, and I have learned a good lesson too—not to do more than I am able."

Gavin discovered that he could do many things that would be of benefit to others, as well as to please himself. He also learned that honest hard work gives a faithful laborer the blessing of a good night's sleep (Ecclesiastes 5:12).

Lesson 42

suddenly—all at once; quickly
mountain—large hill
reached—arrived at
grammar—art of speaking and writing
      correctly
purpose—use; reason
initially—at first; to begin with
quarry—place where stones are dug
bottom—lowest part
science—knowledge
proper—suitable
cease—stop; leave off
use—benefit
built—constructed
hew—cut

The Way to Become Wise

To become wise you must learn many things. At first, you should try to learn only one thing at a time. You may think: "I cannot become as wise as my teacher in a few days, so I will never be able to do so." But this is not right.

No one can become wise suddenly. Even the wisest man in the world, at one time, did not know the alphabet and could not spell or read a word. But he began first to learn his letters, then to spell and read, and so on—learning one thing at a time.

Let me give you an example. If you were going up a mountain, you would not think of trying to step from the bottom to the top, at once! But you would move on—step by step—until you reached the top.

In the same way, you must climb the mountain of "Wisdom". You must first learn to read and spell well; then you can learn to write. After that, you will be able to study grammar and many other useful things.

Sometimes you may say, "I do not see the use of learning this lesson." But you should never say this; because, if you initially do not see the purpose of it, you often will, after you have learned it.

Let me give you another example. If a large, stone house is going to be built, some men need to dig up stones from a quarry; others must cut them into proper shapes. But if these men should stop their work, because they do not know where each stone is to be placed in the house, the house would never be built.

So, if you stop trying to learn your lessons, because you initially cannot see their use, you will never become wise. But, if you are careful—each day of your life—to learn something new and useful, you will become wise and gain the respect of all.

To be wise and good, a person must study the Holy Bible each day to learn how to properly use God's gift of wisdom. The Bible itself states, "The fear of the Lord is the beginning of wisdom." (Psalm 111:10)

LESSON 43

noble—good; first-rate
good-natured—pleasant; friendly
entrusts—hands over; gives
order—command; instruction
although—even if; inspite of
fetch—go and bring back; return with
sneaking—moving quietly
beetle—heavy wooden mallet
fastened—fixed firmly
gnawed—bit; chewed
instead—in place of

The Noble Dog

What a noble dog! What an honest-looking face it has! How good-natured it seems! This dog's name is Buddy. It safely keeps anything that its master entrusts to its care. Its master can even send it to the meat market with a written order for some beef or poultry; Buddy will go alone and bring it home with the greatest care.

See with what care Buddy carries that basket in its mouth! The dog is going home with some poultry! It will bring the poultry for its master's dinner! Buddy's honest-looking face does not mislead you, because the dog will never touch anything put into the basket, although it may be very hungry.

Buddy also has been taught by its master to go from the field to the house to fetch anything the man wanted. One day, the master was at work about a half a mile from home and wanted Buddy to fetch an ax. He told the dog to go to the house and bring him the ax.

Buddy obeyed and started off. After being gone some time, the dog came sneaking back, but it did not bring the ax. Its master again told Buddy to go back and get it. It went the second time; and, after being gone as long as before, it came back with a large beetle in his mouth.

The man then thought the dog could not find the ax, and he went himself and found it fastened in a log. The dog had gnawed the handle from one end to the other, in trying to get it out; but it stuck so firmly that Buddy could not do it. So the dog took the beetle to its master, instead of the ax.

Buddy was kind, obedient, helpful, and always ready to do whatever its master commanded. Even if it was tempted, it did not take what did not belong to it. Such a faithful dog is hard to find. From the conduct of this noble dog, many good lessons may be learned.

LESSON 44

forest—woods; group of trees
chopping—cutting
swiftly—quickly; with great speed
raised—lifted
distress—pain; suffering
at a loss—unable to act; confused
reunion—coming together; meeting
gladness—happiness; joy
treasure—valuable things
welfare—prosperity
ignorant—unaware; not informed
acorns—fruit of the oak
infancy—childhood; early life
shady—sheltered
perils—dangers

The Squirrel's Nest

When Josh was a boy, about nine years of age, he went out into the forest, where his father was chopping wood. In one of the large, hollow trees that he had cut down, Josh found a squirrel's nest with four young ones in it. He took them out of the nest and thought he would take them home as pets.

But his father told Josh to put them back into the nest, since their mother knew how to take care of them much better than Josh did. He obeyed and put them back into the nest. Then he went and hid in the bushes—a little way off—to see what the mother squirrel would do, when she found her house gone.

Soon the mother squirrel came running along, with a nut in her mouth, and went swiftly to the place where the old tree had stood. Finding nothing but a stump, she dropped the nut and began smelling all about the ground. Then she jumped upon the stump to look around. Her babies were nowhere in sight.

She ran around the stump several times and seemed to be in great distress. She then raised herself up on her hind legs, as though at a loss to know what to do. At last, she jumped on the fallen trunk of the tree and ran along until she came to the hole, where she found her little ones all safe in their little warm bed of moss.

What their reunion was like, no one can tell; but no doubt, the mother's heart beat with gladness to find her lost treasure all safe.

After staying with them a short time, she came out and ran off through the bushes; but she soon returned again, took one of the young ones in her mouth, and carried it into a hole in another tree. She then came back and took the others, one by one, in the same way, until she had carried them all safely into their new home.

After that, Josh became concerned about the welfare of his new friends. Whenever he drove the cows to the pasture, he always went by that tree to see how the young family was getting along.

In a short time, the young squirrels were running all over the tree, under the watchful care of their mother. As they ate acorns under the shady boughs, they seemed quite ignorant of the perils they had passed through in their infancy.

LESSON 45

Lily's Happy Home

Now, little girls, and little boys,
What I'm about to say,
Try and remember, at your work,
Your study, or your play.

Lily was a happy child,
As parents ever had;
For she was cheerful all the day;
Her heart was never sad.

Not every home has trees and flowers,
As little Lily's had;
But with the sunshine of the heart,
Your homes may be as glad.

If living in the city grand,
Or in the country wild,
You learn as she, from all you see,
To be a happier child.

Then, if you live in such a place,
As little Lily did,
You'll be yourselves the sweetest flowers,
All sweet and doing good.

Lesson 46

request—plea; petition
burning—very hot
unwillingly—against one's will
crossly—angrily; rudely
kindness—tenderness
thirst—desire drink
coffin—box in which the dead are buried
refused—said no; turned down
pass away—die; expire
comfort—help; cheer
bear—put up with; endure
tempted—enticed to do wrong
bitter—painful
recall—call back
forgiveness—not hold against; pardon

The Last Request

"Ken, will you please bring me a glass of cold water?" asked Anne, as she lay on her pillow, with a burning fever.

But Ken kept on playing his computer game, as though he did not hear her, until he totally forgot her request.

After a few minutes, Anne asked him again for a glass of cold water.

As a result, Ken unwillingly left his game and filled a glass with water, which had been standing out for some time, and gave it to his sister.

When she put it to her burning lips, she turned

her head, and said, "Oh, Ken, please get me some fresh, cool water from the refrigerator."

"Why won't this do?" said Ken crossly. "I am too busy now to go to the kitchen."

So Anne drank the water that Ken brought her; but it was the last time she ever called on him for any small act of kindness.

Before the sun went down that day, she stood beside the River of Life and drank of its cool waters, never to thirst again.

Of all who wept around the coffin of young Anne, there was none that shed more bitter tears than Ken, who could not forget that he had refused the last request of his sister.

Are you kind to each other? Or are you angry or selfish? Remember, the time may come when some of the ones you love will pass away; then, you would be so glad if you could have them back again!

Ken was a kindhearted boy and dearly loved his sister. But since she had been sick only a few days, he did not think she would die so soon. When she was gone, though, this was no comfort to him.

"Oh, Mother!" Ken would say, "if I had only brought that cold water for Anne, I could bear it; but now I can only ask Jesus to forgive me and to take care of Anne until I see her again in heaven."

Think of this story, the next time you are tempted to argue or to be selfish. What if one of your loved ones should die? People may remember the unkind acts or bitter words that had fallen from your lips. But then it would be too late to recall them—too late to ask forgiveness.

LESSON 47

fawn—young deer
adorable—cute; loveable
cuddly—huggable
amused—kept busy; entertained
imaginary—made-up; pretend
pretend—make-up; act as if
real—true; genuine
gratify—please; fulfill
delighted—pleased; happy
creature—living being
attached—united
graceful—elegant
attention—care
outward—outside; external
appearance—what someone looks like
neglect—ignore; disregard
certainly—surely

Jade's Pet Fawn

Jade was a lovely girl, and her father bought her an adorable teddy bear for a present. It was a large, cuddly one with eyes that could open and shut. Jade was very happy with her teddy, and she amused herself for hours at a time, playing all kinds of imaginary games.

But after a while, Jade said, "I am tired of playing with my teddy, because I have to pretend all the time with it.

"I wish I had a real pet of some kind—something that can bark, purr, or sing. I am tired of stuffed animals.

"If I had a little dog or kitten or rabbit to play with, I would have much more fun than I do with this teddy."

Jade had a kind father, who loved his daughter dearly and wanted to gratify her in everything that was proper. So when he heard her make this wish, he brought home an adorable little fawn and gave it to her for a pet.

Jade was delighted with the gentle little creature; and the fawn soon became as much attached to Jade, as she was to it.

When Jade decided to take a walk down the lane, the fawn would throw up its head and bound along beside her.

Jade named her fawn "Little Dear." This was

so because, as she would say, "If my fawn is not a little dear, certainly there never was one."

If a little girl wishes to be graceful as a deer, she must not place too much attention on her outward appearance, and so neglect to care for her heart and mind.

LESSON **48**

lend—let someone use; loan
decide—make up one's mind
borrow—use by permission
secret—something kept from others
convenience—ease; handiness
offended—made to feel bad
resolved—set on; determined

The Lost Pencil

Sandy: Will you lend me your pencil, Sue? Because I can never find mine when I want it.

Sue: And why can you not find yours, Sandy?

Sandy: I am sure I don't know; but if you decide not to lend me yours, I can borrow from somebody else.

Sue: I am willing to lend it to you; but I would like to know why you always come to me to borrow, when you have lost something.

Sandy: Because you never lose your things; you always know where to find them.

Sue: And how do you think I always know where to find my things?

Sandy: How should I know? If I did, sometimes I would be able to find my own things.

Sue: I will tell you the secret, if you will listen. I have a set place for everything. And after I am done using a thing, I always put it in its proper place and never leave it to be thrown about and lost.

Sandy: I never can find time to put my things away. Besides, who wants to run and put them away, as if one's life depended upon it?

Sue: Your life does not depend upon it, Sandy, but your convenience does. Let me ask, how much more time will it take to put a thing in its proper place than to hunt after it, when it is lost? Or to borrow from your friends?

Sandy: Well, Sue, I will never borrow from you again, you may depend upon it.

Sue: Why, Sandy? You are not offended, I hope.

Sandy: No; I am ashamed. But I am also resolved to find a place for everything and to keep everything in its place.

LESSON 49

sleigh—vehicle on runners
afternoon—time between noon and evening
swiftly—quickly; fast
jingle—rattle; tinkle
merrily—cheerfully
bounded—leaped; jumped
cottage—small house
seems—appears
favors—kind acts
least—smallest
relieve—ease; give aid
pity—mercy; kindness
given—presented; bestowed

The Sleigh Ride

One very pleasant Christmas Day, Mr. Scott asked his daughter, Renee, if she would like to take a sleigh ride with him.

"Oh, yes, Father," said Renee; "I would like to go and see that dear old lady, who came to our house last week for some food. She must be very poor!"

"Can't we call on her some other time?" asked her father. "This afternoon, I would like to ride for pleasure."

"I suppose we could," said Renee; "but if you don't mind, I would like to take a basket of food to her. Can we ride around that way, and see how she is getting along?"

"Well, Renee," said Mr. Scott, "we will go and see the poor woman; for we must seek the comfort of others, as well as our own pleasure."

By the time the horse and sleigh were brought to the front door, Renee had filled the basket with food and was all ready to go with her father to see the poor woman.

Mr. Scott had a very swift horse, and it made the bells jingle merrily, as they bounded along over the little hills and valleys.

When they came to the cottage where the poor woman lived, Renee entered and gave her the basket of food.

The woman thanked her for her kindness and said, "I hope you will have a merry Christmas and a happy New Year."

"Thank you for your kind words," said Renee, as she came out and jumped into the sleigh.

While they were riding home, Renee said, "I

really like to help that dear old lady; for she seems to be so thankful for the least favors.

"Besides, the main message of Christmas is how God gave His only Son to relieve the spiritual suffering of man. We also must be willing to give of ourselves to others, just like Jesus did."

"Although I take great pleasure in riding, it gives me greater pleasure to meet the needs of people like this poor woman," said Mr. Scott, in a tearful voice.

"He that has pity on the poor lends to the Lord, and He will pay back what he has given" (Proverbs 19:17).

Lesson 50

stubborn—willful; headstrong
flaw—weak spot; fault
marred—spoiled; impaired
refuse—say "no"; turn down
resolved—set on; determined
dispute—argument; quarrel
thoroughly—completely
screamed—cried out
drenched—wet; soaked
drowned—suffocated in water
humbled—abased
mentioning—talking about
subdue—defeat; overcome
matters—affairs
principle—rule of action
trifles—petty things
yield—give way; give in

The Stubborn Girl and the Goat

Kristen would have been a very good girl, but she had one flaw that marred her life—she was stubborn.

All the girls in school said they would like to play with Kristen, if she were not so willful. If she could have everything done in her own way, she was a very pleasant girl to play with; but, if not, she would refuse to play.

She caused the teacher a great deal of trouble,

because she would even refuse to obey her teacher, if she were told to do anything that she did not want to do.

One day, however, Kristen learned a hard lesson that she did not soon forget.

She had to cross a stream of water on a narrow plank that served as a footbridge. But, just as she stepped on one end, a goat jumped upon the other. Kristen resolved she would not give up to the goat. So they met at the middle of the plank and stood for a few minutes, just staring at each other.

The plank was so narrow that the goat could not turn back and Kristen refused to move. So the goat ended the dispute by pushing Kristen into the water; then it quickly walked over the footbridge.

She screamed for help; but, since no one heard her, she had to get out of the water the best way she could. She was thoroughly drenched and was nearly drowned.

She was greatly humbled. It proved, though, a good lesson for Kristen, because it cured her of her willful conduct.

After this event, when she showed the least sign of being stubborn, only mentioning "the goat on the footbridge" would subdue her at once.

Though we should be firm in matters of duty and principle, yet we should not be stubborn about trifles or too proud to yield when we know we are in the wrong.

LESSON 51

breadcrumbs—small pieces of bread
perch—alight
suddenly—hastily
alarmed—frightened
snatch—grab; steal
prey—food caught by animals
released—set free
destroy—kill
exercise—practice
self-control—control of one's self
control—govern
appetites—desires; longings
revenge—return of injury
desire—want; longing
thirsty—desire for drink
reward—prize; payment

The Cat and the Canary

A lady had a very pretty bird called a canary, which was so tame that she let it come out of its cage and fly around the room to pick up breadcrumbs on the floor.

She also had a large black cat, which she had trained to let the canary perch on its head; and the cat would not disturb it in the least. Indeed, they were real friends.

One morning, the lady opened the cage door to let the bird fly and hop about the room while she was sewing.

The old cat, which lay asleep on the rug, suddenly sprang up, seized the bird in its mouth, and jumped upon the table.

The lady was alarmed for the life of her little canary, and she started from her seat to snatch the bird from the cat's mouth.

Just at that moment, she saw the reason why the cat reacted the way it did. The front door had been left open, and a strange cat had just crept into the room and was about to seize the bird for its prey.

When the lady drove the strange cat out of the house, her own cat leaped from the table and released the little canary, without doing it any harm.

It was the nature of this cat to catch and destroy all the strange birds that came within its reach; but with respect to this little canary, it had learned to exercise self-control.

If children do not learn to control their appetites, great harm may come to them. For, if they eat some fruit, or anything else that they like, and do not control their appetites, they are apt to eat too much and get sick.

Sometimes children get angry at their playmates and seek revenge by doing them harm. But they should learn to control this evil desire. The Bible teaches us to love our enemies and to do good to them that hate us.

It says, "If thine enemy be hungry, give him bread to eat; and if he be thirsty, give him water to drink: for thou shalt heap coals of fire on his head, and the Lord shall reward thee" (Proverbs 25:21-22).

LESSON 52

choice—selection
golden—shining, like gold
hue—color; shade
soar—fly aloft
glitter—shine; sparkle
sparkling—glittering
blossom—bloom
bright—clear; transparent
caroling—singing
fair—comely; beautiful
view—see; behold
shedding—peeling
everywhere—in all places
sincere—honest

Clara's Choice

I would not be a fancy bird,
With wings of golden hue,
That cannot think, or speak a word,
Or learn to read—would you?

I would not be a butterfly,
To soar the bright air through,
Only to glitter, and to die,
And live no more—would you?

I would not be a rosebud gay,
All sparkling in the dew,
Only to blossom for a day,
And give out sweet perfume—would you?

But, like the birds, I would be free,
As bright and happy too,
Caroling still my note of glee,
To cheer the world—wouldn't you?

Or, like the glittering butterfly,
I would be fair to view,
And useful too, that every eye
Might love me—wouldn't you?

Or, like the rose, I would be fair,
And kind and loving too,
Shedding rich fragrance everywhere
For others—wouldn't you?

But, more than all, I would be good,
Sincere, and pure, and true;
And, as I follow my Lord's desires,
Grow wiser—wouldn't you?

LESSON 53

servant—one who serves
ignorant—badly informed
carry—take from one place to another
conceal—hide
theft—act of stealing
denied—said (something) is untrue
finally—lastly
concluded—decided
similar—like
revealed—made known
confessed—admitted (a sin)
errand—task; job
dared—ventured
beholding—seeing

How a Servant Was Cured of Stealing

Here we see Lena and Bob coming home from the library. They are reading about the servant who was cured of stealing.

The story is this: "An ignorant servant, who had never seen any writing, was sent by his master to carry a letter and some oranges to a neighbor lady.

"On the way, the servant ate the oranges. When he gave the letter to the lady, she read it, and then asked him for the oranges.

"He, at first, tried to conceal the theft, by pretending to be ignorant of what she wanted. But she told him that the letter said that his master had sent her some oranges.

"He denied that any had been sent by him. Finally, he concluded that the letter had seen him eat the fruit and had revealed the fact.

"When he was sent again to carry a letter and some oranges to the lady, he hid the letter under a stone, so it would not see him eat the oranges.

"He then took the letter from under the stone and carried it to the lady, who, after reading it, asked him for the oranges. Then he confessed he had eaten them.

"After that, when he was sent on a similar errand, he dared not steal; for he thought that the letter knew and revealed his wicked conduct."

If you should ever be tempted to steal, or deceive by telling a falsehood, I hope you will call to mind the story of this ignorant servant.

Although you know that the letter could not see nor reveal what the servant did, yet you should remember there is One who sees and knows all you think or do.

"The eyes of the Lord are in every place, beholding the evil and the good" (Proverbs 15:3); and "He knoweth the secrets of the heart" (Psalm 44:21).

LESSON 54

conqueror—one who overcomes
exclaimed—cried out; shouted
thousands—tens of hundreds
conquer—overcome; defeat
kernel—seed; embryo
warrior—fighter; soldier
defeated—conquered
flee—run away; escape
discouraged—downcast; saddened
defeats—losses; setbacks
resolved—made up his mind; decided
cell—small room; chamber
reached—came to
seized—grabbed hold of
courage—daring; guts
successful—winning; victorious
succeed—do well; make it
effort—struggle; power
heed—listen to carefully
patience—staying power

The Little Conqueror

"Oh, Mother!" exclaimed Mark, "I will never learn this lesson; it is so hard! I am going to quit!"

"You are going to quit?" asked his mother. "Son, never let it be said that a lesson, which thousands of other children have learned, will conquer you."

"But, Mother," argued Mark, "I have read this lesson more than twenty times, and I still don't understand it!"

"Yes, Son," said his mother, "but you have not tried half as many times as the little ant, which tried over and over again to get a little kernel of corn into its home."

"Why, Mother," asked Mark, "how many times did it try? Please tell me the story."

"The story is this," said his mother:

"Timur was a great warrior; but he was defeated several times by his enemies. In the end, he was forced to flee and hide in an old building.

"He was very discouraged by his defeats, and he almost resolved to never try to conquer his enemies again.

"One day, he saw a little ant trying to get a kernel of corn into its cell, which was close to the top of the wall. But just before it reached its cell, its strength failed, and the ant fell to the floor.

"But the little ant did not give up. It seized hold of the kernel of corn and tried again; and the ant fell to the floor the second time.

"Over and over again, the ant went on trying sixty-nine times, and it fell to the floor every time; but, on the seventieth time, the ant reached the cell with its prize.

"The conduct of the ant gave Timur courage to try again to conquer his enemies; and, in the end, he was successful. After that, he never forgot the lesson he learned from the little ant."

"Hooray for the little ant and the great warrior,

too!" exclaimed Mark. "I will succeed with my lesson, as the ant succeeded with the kernel of corn. I will not give up! I will conquer it!"

After a little effort, Mark understood his lesson. He learned it thoroughly. After that, he hardly ever failed to conquer his lessons, because he always remembered the words of his mother: "It is always too soon to give up."

'Tis a lesson you should heed,
Try, try again;
If, at first, you don't succeed,
Try, try again:

All that other folks can do,
Why, with patience, may not you?
Only keep this rule in view—
Try, try again.

Lesson 55

apply—use; employ
apart—at a distance
course—line; row
next—nearest
raise—lift; move up
in vain—with little hope
mankind—people; human beings
rejoice—be glad
promote—uphold; advance
welfare—good; well-being

Brian and the Bricks

One day, Brian heard his father say, "This is a poor rule that won't work both ways." But Brian thought if his father could apply this rule to his work, then he would try it with bricks. Brian wanted to see if it was a poor rule.

So Brian set up a long row of bricks, four or five inches apart. Then he tipped over the first brick, which struck against the second, and caused it to fall against the third; and so on, through the whole course, until all the bricks had fallen.

"Well," said Brian, "each brick has knocked down the one that stood next to it; but I only tipped one. Now I will raise one, and see if it will raise all the rest." But he looked in vain to see them rise.

"Yes, Father," said Brian, "this is a poor rule, because it will not work both ways. The bricks knock each other down, but they will not raise each other up."

"My son," said the father, "in some respects, your bricks and mankind are very much alike. They are both made of clay and are more active in knocking each other down, than they are in helping each other up.

"When men fall, some people like to have others fall too; but when they rise, they like to stand alone, and see others fall.

"The Bible says, 'The poor is hated even of his own neighbor; but the rich hath many friends' (Proverbs 14:20).

"Son, we should never rejoice at the difficulties of others, but we should try to promote the welfare and happiness of our neighbors."

Lesson 56

hornet—large wasp
mischievous—doing mischief
mischief—harm
fiercely—angrily; violently
thrust—push with force
rushed—moved quickly
agony—extreme pain
punished—disciplined; chastised
mercy—compassion
swollen—puffed-up
companions—friends
righteous—just
regardeth—valueth

Peter and the Hornet's Nest

Peter was a mischievous boy, and he caused himself and others a great deal of trouble. He was very bright, but he seemed to take more pleasure in doing mischief than in doing good.

One day, he found a hornet's nest in some bushes that stood at the edge of the pasture, in which some cattle and horses were feeding.

If you have never seen a hornet's nest, it is shaped nearly round, like a football; and it hangs on the limb of a tree or bush. It has a hole at the bottom, through which the insects pass in and out.

Hornets are much larger than honeybees; and they have powerful stings and fight fiercely when anyone disturbs their nest.

So, on this terrible day, Peter thrust a stick into their nest; then he ran and hid in the thick bushes, where the hornets could not find him. In this way, he made them very angry.

Next, he took some salt and spread it on the grass, near the hornet's nest; and then he called the cattle and horses to lick it up.

As soon as they began to lick the salt, Peter threw a club against the nest. The angry hornets rushed out and fiercely stung the cattle and horses.

The animals ran, bellowing and kicking, around the pasture, as though they would kill themselves. This was very cruel, and yet it was foolish fun for this wicked boy.

But Peter was justly punished for his cruel conduct. He was so pleased to see the poor cattle and horses kick and bellow in agony that he jumped out of the bushes, laughing and shouting very loudly.

But his joy was soon turned to fear, because some of the hornets saw him coming out of the bushes. Immediately, they flew at him and stung his face and neck, causing him to cry for mercy.

He ran home as fast as he could, but his face was so swollen by the stings of the hornets that he could hardly see for many days.

Peter did not receive much pity from his young companions, for they all had heard how he came to be stung so badly.

The Bible says, "A righteous man regardeth the life of his beast; but the tender mercies of the wicked are cruel" (Proverbs 12:10).

Lesson 57

boarding school—school where students live, as well as study
village—rural community; town
ponies—small horses
pupils—students; learners
failed—were not able
seldom—not often; rarely
developed—used; built on
approaching—coming near
whistle—shrill sound
startled—upset; troubled
cantered—quickly trotted; nearly galloped
might—strength; power
manage—control; handle
describing—telling; recounting
delightful—pleasing; enjoyable
incidents—events; happenings
transpired—taken place

The Ride on the Ponies

Mr. Bennett taught at a boarding school, in a pleasant village near the banks of the Hudson River. He kept little ponies for his pupils to ride out into the country, when the weather was pleasant. Mr. Bennett also kept a fine large horse for his own use; and, when his pupils rode out, he always went with them.

If any of the pupils failed to complete their lessons, or did not act in a proper manner, Mr. Bennett would not allow them to ride on his ponies. As the pupils were all very fond of riding, they seldom failed in their lessons, and always tried to behave in a proper manner.

Mr. Bennett taught his pupils to do their best, even if no earthly reward—such as riding on ponies—was offered. They began to understand that knowledge was a gift in itself. They also learned that this gift should be developed, not wasted.

One afternoon, as they were riding near some railroad tracks, they saw a train with a number of cars approaching. Mr. Bennett immediately commanded, "Turn at the next corner, and ride up the hill. I am afraid that your ponies will be frightened."

Soon after they turned the corner, the whistle of the engine blew. It startled the ponies so much that they cantered up the hill with all their might.

But Mr. Bennett had taught his pupils how to manage the ponies when they became frightened, so that the pupils were not afraid of being thrown off and hurt.

When the riding party came to the top of the hill, they turned the ponies around to look at the train as it passed. Then they returned home.

After some snacks, they wrote letters to their friends, describing the delightful ride and the incidents that had transpired. They truly enjoyed their outing.

Lesson 58

geography—study of the earth
recite—say; repeat
earth—planet we live on
globe—round body
map—chart
planet—heavenly body; globe
proof—evidence
shadow—shaded part; outline
surface—outer part; crust
rotates—turns on its axis
axis—made-up line through the center of
      earth
revolves—turns or moves around
appear—seem
opposite—other; reverse
direction—course; way
different—unlike
seasons—divisions of the year

A Lesson in Geography

Susan: Mother, will you please listen to me recite my lesson?

Mother: Yes, Susan; let me see your book.

What is the shape of the earth?

Susan: It is round, like a globe or ball.

Mother: How do you know that the earth is round?

Susan: Well, it looks as though it were round, on the map.

Mother: Yes; but the map is only a picture of the earth; and the picture may be wrong.

Susan: Well, the book says that the earth is round, because many astronauts have traveled around our planet and viewed it from outerspace.

Mother: Yes; that is one proof that the earth is round; and another is that the shadow of the earth on the moon is round; and if the shadow is round, the earth must be round.

How much of the earth's surface is land?

Susan: About one fourth is land; the rest is water.

Mother:	Can you tell how far it is around the earth?
Susan:	Yes; it is about twenty-five thousand miles.
Mother:	Does the earth move?
Susan:	Yes; it rotates, or turns on its axis, from west to east; this takes place once every twenty-four hours. This makes day and night.
Mother:	How do you know that the earth revolves in this manner?
Susan:	Because, the sun, moon, and stars all appear to move from east to west. If the earth revolved in the opposite direction, from east to west, they would all appear to move from west to east.
Mother:	Yes; as you ride along in the car, the trees and houses appear to move in an opposite direction from which you are going. It is just same with the sun, moon, and stars.
	Does the earth move in any other way?
Susan:	Yes; it revolves around the sun, once every year, which causes the different seasons—spring, summer, autumn, and winter.

LESSON 59

tiny—small; little
awhile—a short time
threw—cast; flung
carelessly—without care
round—circle or circuit
sturdy—stout; hardy
fiercest—most violent
defy—dare; brave
uproot—tear up; upturn
habits—customs; practices

The Boy and the Acorn

A very little boy once found
A tiny acorn on the ground;
Awhile he held it in his play,
Then threw it carelessly away.

Winters and summers ran their round,
And now on that same spot is found
A sturdy oak, whose branches high,
The winter's fiercest storms defy.

The child who threw the acorn there,
Has been a man this many a year;
But though a large, strong man is he,
He never could uproot that tree.

And so 'tis with our habits strong;
They grow, each day, for right or wrong;
And he who forms them as he should,
Will see that every one is good.

LESSON 60

mussels—small shellfish
northern—being in the north
coast—shoreline
strewn—spread; scattered
beaks—bills
way—means; methods
method—way; manner
truly—really
worthy—deserving
notice—attention
obtained—got a hold of; took
unwise—foolish; hasty
remark—comment; statement
accomplished—get done; achieved

The Crows and the Mussels

As a man was traveling on the northern coast of Ireland, he saw more than a hundred crows trying to break open the mussel shells that lay strewn along the shore. Finding the shells too hard to break with their beaks, they decided to open their shells in some other way. Their new method was truly worthy of notice.

Each crow took a mussel up in the air, about 100 feet, and then let it fall on the stones, breaking the shell. In this way, the crow easily obtained the mussel's flesh.

Can you learn anything from these crows?

If you were told to do something, and you said,

"I can't do it"—even before you had tried—this would be a very unwise remark. But if you tried one more time, the thing may be accomplished; however, if this should fail, it may be done in some other way. Never say, "I can't do it."

The crows that could not open the shells with their beaks, broke them by dropping the shells and getting the mussels' flesh; likewise, if you are told to do anything, you should not give up until every possible solution has been tried.

Lesson 61

tend—take care of; look after
purchase—buy
plucked—pulled
in spite of—in defiance of
selfishness—self-love
humility—freedom from pride
vanity—pride; self-conceit
industry—diligence
germs—seed-bud
ugly—not pleasant to look at
thrive—grow; increase
showy—gaudy
violet—dark blue flower
hurtful—injurious
idleness—laziness
noxious—harmful
thrive—grow freely
passions—emotions

The Little Flower Garden

Paul and Karen had a little garden of their own, which their father allowed them to plant and tend. He told them that they must pull out all the weeds and do all they could to help the plants grow. Their father also gave them some money and told them to purchase flower seeds to plant in their garden.

When the little germs began to poke out of the ground, Paul and Karen watered them every day; and, as the plants grew, they were careful to keep them free from weeds and insects. They also made a nice gravel walk around their flowerbed, which they kept quite smooth and clean.

Each day, when their mother had finished teaching them, they would run into the garden to look at their beautiful flowers. With all this care, their flowerbed looked very pretty. But the weeds gave them a great deal of trouble. It seemed that, as fast as they were plucked up in one place, they grew in another.

"I do not like those ugly weeds," said Karen to her mother. "They must not grow in my garden; I want only beautiful flowers to be there."

"Yes," said Paul, "I am sure we have tried our best to keep them out; but they will still grow in spite of all we can do."

"It is just like some other little gardens," said their mother, "in which I would like to see only beautiful flowers grow. But, I am sorry to say, I have seen many noxious weeds thrive there; though great pains have been taken to keep them out.

"I have often thought I could see a few buds; but they have not come into full blossom. And, sometimes, where I hoped to find a flower, I have only plucked a weed."

"What little gardens are you talking about, Mother?" asked Karen.

"They are the gardens of your young hearts, my children," said their mother. "You know I have desired to see nothing grow there but pleasant flowers.

"One of these is 'kindness'; and a very large and pretty plant it is when full-grown. But the weeds of 'selfishness' too often spring up around it, until it is almost covered from my view.

"'Humility' is a very lovely flower. It does not show off, because—like the sweet violet—it hides itself among its own leaves. It is a sweet-smelling blossom.

"But there are tall and showy weeds, called 'pride' and 'vanity,' which—though pleasing to some—are very harmful to the flowers.

"'Truth' is another plant in these gardens; but the cruel weed of 'falsehood' will come up by its side and cause it soon to wither and die.

"Then there are other flowers known by the names of 'industry' and 'peace,' which are very beautiful; but the weeds of 'idleness' and 'anger' often choke the plants, before they are fully grown."

"Oh, Mother! Now I know what you mean," said Paul. "The flowers are good passions and noble conduct, and the weeds are our wicked passions and evil conduct."

"You are right, Paul; and you and your sister should know that the soil of your hearts is friendly to the growth of these hurtful weeds.

"So you must strive to root out, and subdue these noxious weeds; and then I shall see in you those flowers, which are the most lovely that can be found in the human heart."

Lesson 62

marriage—a covenant or promise
special—unusual or unique
welcome—gladly accept
teach—educate

Marriage

After God made the world, He made a man named Adam. God saw that the man needed a friend and a helper to live with him, so God made a woman named Eve to be a wife for Adam. God saw that this was very good. Adam and Eve lived together and took care of each other. This was the first marriage.

Marriage is very special. God thought of the idea Himself, because He knew that it would be good for us, and that we would like it.

When a man finds a woman that he wants to live with all of his life, he must ask the woman and her parents if he may marry her. If the parents say yes, the man and the woman marry on a special day called a wedding day.

After that, they live together just like Adam and Eve. God says they must always live together until they die. Marriage is a lifelong promise.

Usually God will bless the man and woman with children. They will be glad and welcome the children into their family. The man and the woman will take care of the children, teach them about God and His love, and everything else they will need to know.

Marriage is so special because that is the way God continues to fill the earth with His people.

LESSON 63

senses—ways we understand things around us
smelled—sniffed; sensed
blindfold—cover eyes with a cloth
introduce—bring in
visitor—guest
cousin—child of an uncle or aunt
handkerchief—cloth used for the face
discovery—finding; uncovering
deceived—misled; tricked

The Five Senses

Sam: Father, I have heard some people say
         we have five senses; and I asked a friend
         what they are, and he said he could not

tell. I then asked my cousin, and he said we have four senses—walking, talking, eating, and drinking. Is it so? Do tell me.

Father: You have just been telling me how beautiful the country looked, covered with snow, as we were riding through it a few days ago. How did you know it?

Sam: Well, Father, I saw it with my eyes.

Father: Could you know anything, if you did not have eyes, Sam?

Sam: I don't think so, Father. It would be like the night, when it is so dark; it seems as if there were nothing around me.

Father: Shut your eyes. There, now; tell me, is this footstool hard or soft?

Sam: The footstool is hard, Father.

Father: How do you know that it is hard, when your eyes are shut?

Sam: I cannot see it; but I know it, because I touched it.

Father: You can know something in two ways, then—by sight and touch. Now shut your eyes again, and put your hands behind you. What is this I have put under your nose?

Sam: Father, it is a rose!

Father:	But how do you know it is a rose, when you have neither seen nor felt it?
Sam:	Well, I smelled it; nothing smells so sweet! Oh, Father, there are three ways of knowing things—by seeing, feeling, and smelling!
Father:	I will now blindfold you with this handkerchief, so that you cannot see, even if you want to. There, do you see now?
Sam:	No, Father, I cannot see anything.
Father:	Now, put one hand behind you, and hold your nose with the other. Now you cannot see, feel, nor smell. I will now introduce a visitor to you. Come here, my friend, and wish Sam good evening.
Anna:	Good evening, Sam.
Sam:	Good evening, Anna.
Father:	Ha! How do you know this is Anna?
Sam:	Because I heard her speak; don't you think I can tell my sister's voice?
Father:	Very well; here, then, is a new discovery. Now do you know how many ways there are of knowing things?
Sam:	Four—seeing, feeling, smelling, and hearing.
Father:	Anna, place your hands over Sam's ears; then we shall see if there is another way

of knowing things. Open your mouth. What have I put into it?

Sam: A piece of chocolate.

Father: How do you know that it is chocolate?

Sam: I tasted it with my tongue; I am quite a good judge of tasty treats like chocolate.

Father: Your taste has not deceived you. But what new way have you found of knowing things?

Sam: By my taste.

Father: Now, my son, you have discovered five ways we can gain knowledge of things; and they are seeing, feeling, smelling, hearing, and tasting. These are called the five senses.

LESSON 64

dealt—traded
dealers—traders
steadily—constantly
defects—faults
future—time to come
proved—was found to be
desire—wish
trusty—faithful
confidence—trust; reliance
customers—purchasers
market hours—time for trading
decreasing—becoming less
dishonest—lying; deceitful
purchased—bought
earned—gained
prospects—objects in view
merchant—dealer
decided—made up one's mind

The Two Market Boys

Two boys came to a market early in the morning and set up their food stands; then they stood waiting for customers. Eric sold melons and other fruits, and John dealt in oysters and fish.

The market hours passed along quickly and the young dealers saw, with delight, their items steadily decreasing, while the money was filling their pockets.

The last melon lay on Eric's stand, when a gentleman came along, and, placing his hand upon it, said, "What a fine, large melon! I think I will buy it. What are you asking for it, my boy?"

"That melon is the last I have, sir; and though it looks very fair, there is a bad spot on the other side," said Eric, turning it over.

"So there is," said the man. "I think I will not take it. But," said he, looking at Eric, "is it very business-like to point out the defects of your fruit to customers?"

"I think it is better than to be dishonest, sir," said Eric.

"You are right, my boy," said the man; "always speak the truth, and you will find favor with God and man. You have nothing else I could buy this morning; but I shall not forget your fruit stand in the future."

The gentleman then passed along to John's stand, and said, "You have some very fine-looking oysters, my boy. Are they fresh?"

"Yes, sir," said John; "they were fresh this morning." The gentleman purchased a dozen oysters, and went home.

After the man had gone, John turned to Eric, and said, "What a fool you were, to show the gentleman that spot in the melon! Don't you realize how much money you have lost?

"What does he know about those oysters? I sold them at the same price I did the fresh ones. He never would have looked at the melon, until he had gone away."

"I would neither tell a lie, nor act one, for twice what I have earned this morning," said Eric. "Besides, I shall be richer in the end; for I have gained a customer, and you have lost one."

And so it proved to be true. The next day, the gentleman bought quite a supply of fruit from Eric; but he never spent another penny at John's stand.

The gentleman found that he could get a good and fair deal from Eric. Therefore, he always bought from him; and sometimes talked a few minutes with him about his future hopes and prospects.

Eric had a great desire to be a merchant. When the winter came, the gentleman wanted a trusty boy for his store, and he decided to give the job to Eric. He steadily won the confidence of his employer; and, in the end, he became one of the partners in the firm.

Lesson 65

draw—sketch; describe
infant—baby; young child
observed—saw; noticed
intended—meant; designed
represent—show; portray
resembled—looked a lot like
natural—real; genuine
accuracy—correctness; exactness
improving—getting better

An American Painter

Benjamin West was a boy who liked to draw pictures. One day, his mother asked him to rock the cradle, in which his infant brother was sleeping, while she went to visit one of her neighbors.

While rocking the cradle, he observed his brother very closely and was pleased to see the baby smile in his sleep.

Seeing a piece of paper, pen, and ink lying on the table, he began to draw a picture of the smiling infant.

When his mother came home, he asked her not to be angry with him for taking the pen, ink, and paper; then he showed her the picture he had made.

His mother knew at once what the picture was intended to represent. She kissed her dutiful boy and told him he had done well.

She was so pleased with his first effort that she told him he should try to draw a picture of some flowers that stood in a vase.

He drew them with much accuracy and painted them so well that they almost resembled the natural flowers.

As each day went by, Benjamin kept on improving; until at last, he became one of the finest painters in the world.

What Benjamin West could do, other young boys and girls could do as well, if they would only spend their time developing their God-given talents.

Children would also do well to listen to the wishes of their parents. Mr. West was often heard to say, "My mother's kiss made me a painter."

Lesson 66

We're Having a Baby!

Hi! I'm Susie. That's my mom. She's going to have a baby. She has another baby—that's me. Really, I am bigger now; I am five years old.

This is the room where the baby will sleep after he or she is born. This is the same spot that I slept in when I was a baby.

Mom says that babies are God's special gift. Father and Mother and I asked God to give us one, and He is going to. The baby is growing inside Mother now. God has a very special place for the baby to stay until it is time for him or her to be born.

The baby could be a boy baby or a girl baby. Mother says it doesn't matter because either way the baby will be God's gift to our family.

One day we will choose a name for our baby. That is important because he or she will be called by that name his whole life.

When the baby is born, he will need lots of help. Mother and I will give him baths and dress him. We will talk to him and sing to him songs about Jesus and how much Jesus loves us. Mother will feed him.

Sometimes she will have to be up with him during the night. The baby will need Mother's help a lot. Mother says we will have to take care of the baby because he will not be able to take care of himself. Babies need lots of help to grow.

I will help him grow up safe and strong. I am glad God is going to give us a baby. Perhaps Mother will let me hold the baby after he is born.

LESSON 67

The Family

A family is very special. God made the first family; He made Adam and Eve. God also blessed them with many children; their first two were Cain and Abel.

In a family there is love. This is the way God wants it to be. A family is a place to feel happy and secure. A family also has fun together; they play and enjoy being with each other. A family works together, too; everyone helps to get things done.

In a family, God puts the father in charge. This is the way God designed things. The mother is the father's helper. She is in charge if the father is not home. But God gave the father the job of providing food for the family and a place for them to live. It is his job to protect the family from ideas and people that might hurt it.

God gave the mother the job of having babies and caring for her children. It is also her job to care for the home—the place where they live—to keep it tidy, clean, and cheerful.

Most of all, God gave both the father and mother the job of teaching their children. The parents must teach their children all they will need to know about life, especially about Jesus and His love. The most important thing that parents must teach their children is how to love and serve the Lord Jesus Christ.

The Bible commands, "Honour thy father and thy mother" (Exodus 20:12, Deuteronomy 5:16). Thus, it is important to honor your father and mother. This means you should love them, listen to them, and do what they tell you to do. You also should not speak badly about your father and mother to others.

Your family will only be happy if all of you live like the Bible tells you to live. God promises that if you honor your parents—and your parents honor God and the Bible—then you will live a long time on the earth. You, like all children, should be thankful to God for your family.

Lesson 68

toe the mark—follow the rules
occur—take place; happen
favorite—most wanted
rather—more willingly; sooner
formed—arranged
company—group; band
marching—moving in order
office—position; duty
corporal—low ranking officer
duty—job; responsibility
constantly—all the time
important—necessary; essential
declared—stated; affirmed
exactly—just so; correctly
consistently—with out fail
skillful—clever; skilled
trusted—depended on
required—necessary; demanded
special—unique; particular

Learn to Toe the Mark

Lyman Foster was a quiet young boy with a smiling face, who, at first sight, won the respect of all who knew him. He was a good-natured boy; and seldom did anything occur to remove the pleasant smile from his face.

And yet, he was not the favorite boy to play with at school. Most of the boys would rather play with any other boy.

One day, Thomas Benton had formed a company of young soldiers, and he was marching them around the town square with a great deal of pride.

Lyman Foster wanted to join the company, and he felt very proud, when he was raised to the office of corporal.

But he did not do his duty. Captain Benton was constantly finding fault with him. "Corporal Foster," he would ask, "why don't you toe the mark?"

Corporal Foster gave a good-natured smile, but he did not seem to think it important to do what he had been told.

This caused the captain to run out of patience; and he declared that he would not have a man in his company who would not obey orders. So the company was broken up.

While all the other boys were upset, Corporal Foster was as cheerful as ever, and thought it strange that the others did not like to train with him. The trouble was that he would not "toe the mark."

So it was in all their games. The boys did not like to play with Corporal Foster, since he never really tried to do anything exactly as it should be done. He was consistently careless.

When he went to school, he seldom took the time to do his lessons well. A few years later, Lyman Foster dropped out of school to learn a trade; but he never became a skillful workman.

He never could be trusted to do any work that required special care, because he did not learn to "toe the mark" when he was young.

Lesson 69

perfect—complete; no mistakes
ripening—maturing
pod—seed case; shell
skillfully—with great skill
lining—inner cover
polished—made smooth
tight—close; snug
closed—shut; fastened
exposed—laid open
disorder—mess; confusion
anywhere—in any place
condescends—humbles oneself
precious—valuable; important

The Works of God, Perfect

How neatly all the seeds are laid
Within the ripening pod!
How skillfully they, too, are made!
This is the work of God.

The lining is not harsh or rough;
But soft and polished well;
Each little seed has room enough
Within its tiny cell.

How very tight the sides are closed
Against the wind and rain!
For, if the seeds were left exposed,
They would not grow again.

There's no disorder anywhere
In what my Father does;
He condescends to make with care
The smallest flower that grows.

Let children who would learn from Him,
Neat habits seek to gain;
Or they will waste much precious time,
And do their work in vain.

sign—token; evidence
miser—greedy, stingy person
hoarding—hiding away
disputing—arguing
quarrelsome—ready to pick a fight
drunkard—one who gets drunk
obedient—dutiful
profane—wicked; not righteous
shunned—avoided
character—peculiar qualities of a person
loath—against; unwilling
spendthrift—person who wastes
passionate—revengeful
filthy—dirty; impure
pauper—poor person
regard—look upon
vulgar—low; obscene
despised—scorned
general—universal

Signs That Seldom Fail

Solomon, the wisest man that ever lived, has said, "Even a child is known by his doings, whether his work be pure, and whether it be right" (Proverbs 20:11). Boys and girls, even while they are very young, often show signs of what they are likely to be when they become men and women.

If boys or girls try to find some excuse to neglect their schooling, perhaps it is a sign that they will not be successful.

If a child always saves things for himself and is

unwilling to share with others, perhaps it is a sign that he will become a selfish person.

If a child hoards his pennies and is unwilling to part with them for any good purpose, perhaps it is a sign that he will be a miser.

If a child spends all his money as soon as he gets it, perhaps it is a sure sign that he will be a spendthrift.

If boys and girls often dispute and quarrel with each other, perhaps it is a sign that they will become impatient and quarrelsome men and women.

If a child smokes cigarettes, or chews tobacco, perhaps it is a sign that he will soon be guilty of other bad habits.

If boys and girls do not obey their parents, perhaps it is a sign that they will not enjoy a long and happy life.

If a child uses profane or ungodly language, perhaps it is a sign that he will be shunned and despised by all good persons.

If a child takes small things that do not belong to him, perhaps it is a sign that he will become a thief.

If a child spends his time in idleness, when he should be at study or work, perhaps it is a sign that he will become a lazy man.

These signs have been observed by all; and, as a general rule, they seldom fail. But, this is not always true. By God's grace, great and wonderful changes sometimes take place in the character of boys and girls.

Lesson 71

curious—interested
watched—observed
thither—to that place
weary—tired
profit—benefit
patiently—carefully
constructing—building
fabric— structure
hither—to this place
whenever—at whatever time
guessed—supposed
whatever—all that
tiresome—wearisome

The Boy and the Robin

A little boy happened, one morning, to see
A robin constructing her nest on a tree;
The fabric so curious she just had begun,
So he watched her, each day, till the work was all done.

Hither and thither, and around and around,
Now on the branches, and now on the ground,
The little bird flew; but, whenever she came,
She brought something back her new fabric to frame.

"I wonder she never stops even to rest,"
The little boy thought; but the robin knew best;
And, if she was weary, 'twas not very long,
Or she could not have sung such a sweet, cheerful song.

The little boy watched her with patience, each day,
Until she no longer kept flying that way;
And then, pretty soon, ah! what did he see?
Four little blue eggs in the nest on the tree.

The boy did not take them; but, ah! by and by,
There came from the nestlings a weak, tiny cry,
Such sweet little tones he had ne'er before heard,
And he guessed that they came from a dear little bird.

The boy guessed aright; for there, by and by,
The old bird was teaching the young ones to fly;
For she knew the cold winter would come, and that they
To a warm, sunny country, must soon fly away.

The little boy learned, and so may all we,
A lesson of profit from the bird on the tree:
He learned that, whatever our hands find to do,
We must patiently toil till our labor is through.

That little by little, and so every one
Should toil at his task till his work is all done;
And that, though the labor be tiresome and long,
We can make it quite pleasant by a sweet, cheerful song.
So the little boy acted on this noble plan,
And he grew up to be a wise and good man.

Lesson 72

without—outwardly
within—inwardly
fully—entirely
dangerous—not safe
heavenly—of heaven
fraught—filled; full
trust—have faith
serve—worship
eternity—for ever

The Child's Prayer

1. Father, hear me from above,
Guard me with Thine arms of love;
Keep me safe from every sin,
Pure without, and pure within,
Let, oh let no evil word
From my lips be ever heard!
Let, oh let my heart be fraught
With no vain or idle thought!
Keep my soul from folly free;
Let me fully trust in Thee.

2. Help me to be kind and true,
Gentle, pure, and faithful too;
Guard me from the tempter's power;
Save me in each dangerous hour;
Keep me in the path of truth;
Let me serve Thee while in youth;
And when life's short race is o'er,
Lead me to the heavenly shore,
Where all hearts from sin are free,
Happy through eternity.

LESSON 73

affairs—business; concerns
homeward—towards home
simply—just; only
gaudy—flashy; colorful

Secrets of Nature

Dear little squirrel! won't you tell
How you can pick a nut so well,
With no hammer to break the shell?
The squirrel answered not at all,
But slipped into the old stone wall.

Beautiful butterfly! I wish I knew
Who gave those silken wings to you,
And painted them with every hue!
'Tis useless to ask the gaudy things,
How they came by their painted wings.

Diligent bee! I must ask you
How you make cells so neat and true,
And draw from flowers clear honey dew?
The busy bee buzzed no reply,
But with his load he hurried by.

God's little creatures, ev'ry one,
Know how their own affairs are done,
And what to seek and what to shun;
But they can't teach us to make a nest;
Nor could they guide us in distress.

There's much that we can never know,
Of things above and things below;
Simply because God wills it so.
How angels live, there's none can say;
Nor how bees homeward find their way.

We only know that God above,
Who formed the eagle and the dove,
Created all with wisest love;
And gave due wisdom unto each,
Better than all that man can teach.

fiercest—most violent
restore—bring back
annoy—upset; disturb
recorded—written
promoted—raised in rank
bemoan—complain about
ward off—repel; keep off

The Little Soldier

"Oh, I wish I were a soldier!"
Cried little Herbert Lee:
"If I were only older,
How very brave I'd be!
I'd fear not any danger,
I'd flee not from the foe;
But, where the strife was fiercest,
There I'd be sure to go.

"I'd be the boldest hero,
Nor fear the darkest night;
Could I but see a traitor,
How bravely I would fight!
I'd nobly do my duty,
And soon promoted be,
Oh, I wish I were a soldier!"
Sighed little Herbert Lee.

"But, when I'm grown to manhood,
This war will all be o'er;
I cannot join the struggle
Our dear flag to restore.
I may not bleed for freedom,
That glory's not for me;
My name will not be written,
The hero, Herbert Lee!"

Then answered Herbert's mother,
In tender, loving tone,
"My darling little Herbert,
You need not thus bemoan;
A noble strife awaits you,
'T's even now begun,
And you may gain the victory,
If brave and true, my son.

You are a little soldier,
A Christian one, my boy,
To ward off every evil
That may your soul annoy.
The noblest of all soldiers
My little son may be,
His name in Heaven recorded,
The hero, Herbert Lee!"

LESSON 75

hooray—shout of gladness
gentle—mild; peaceful
often—frequent event
angry—upset; mad
echo—sound that returns to its sender

A Voice in the Woods

Jim was playing all by himself in a field near a forest. He was so happy that he called out, "Hooray! Hooray!"

A voice from the woods said, "Hooray! Hooray!"

Jim thought the voice came from a boy in the woods. He looked around, but he could not see anyone. Then he called out, "Who are you?"

"Who are you?" said the voice.

"What is your name?" called Jim.

"What is your name?" came back from the woods.

Jim was getting angry. So he called out at the top of his voice, "You are a goose."

Back came the voice, "You are a goose."

Jim then became very angry. He looked everywhere; no one was to be seen. So he went home and told his father that someone in the woods had called him names.

"Did he speak first?" asked his father.

"No," said Jim. "I was just calling 'Hooray!' and he began to say 'Hooray!' too. I could not see him, so I asked 'Who are you?' Then he called out 'Who are you?' and everything I said he said after me."

"There was only one boy there, Jim," said his father, "and that was you. What you heard today was the echo of your voice. If you had used kind and gentle words, you would have heard kind and gentle words from the echo."

"This was the echo from the woods, Jim. But you will often hear an echo from your friends. They will speak to you as you do to them. Try always to speak to them as you wish them to speak to you. After all, some day you will stand before the Lord Jesus Christ and hear every word you spoke during your life come echoing back."